Rising Crest of the Dragon

A Sir Notalot Adventure

by

Stefan Gadnell

* * * * *

*****

I hope you enjoy my little story
as much as I enjoyed getting it into print.

*****

Rising Crest of the Dragon - A Sir Notalot Adventure
Translated from Swedish by Petra Jannhans

ISBN: 978-91-989402-2-0

Chapter 1:
The First Steps

The dragon slept soundly in his cave, as content dragons often do. The more treasures a dragon has, the better it feels. This dragon had a lot of gold, silver, precious stones, and jewellery. The entire cavern was as large as a church, and the floor was covered with gold coins and other valuables, all scattered in a messy heap. He had also recently managed to steal a beautiful princess, which gave him the feeling of possessing something exceptionally valuable.

The girl sat quietly in a cage hanging in the back of the hall. This was an optimal fortune, the dragon thought, nothing was missing. He felt good, very good, as he slept on top of his mountain of gold.

There was a slight clinking sound from the coins when he rolled onto his back and put his arms behind his head. The storm outside did not bother him; the cave narrowed and led to a sturdy gate that shut out all wind and rain. Now and then, he could hear a faint rumble of thunder; that was all he noticed of the storm. No one could enter and disturb the dragon who preferred to be inside his cave, cozying up amongst his treasures.

The dragon's name was Art, actually Artemisia Dracunculus, but that was too long to think about and say, so he always called himself Art. He was old, so old that no living person could remember where he came from, hardly even he himself. For the last hundred years, he had guarded his treasure in the cave in Mount Dragon and rarely left its gates.

He was green and as big as a horse, which was normal for his kind. It may seem small, but dragons are not larger; it's all those exaggerated stories that have made everyone believe dragons are as big as dinosaurs. His hind legs were strong, his tail as thick as a tree trunk, but his arms and wings were quite weak. They had worked when he was young, but since he hadn't flown in the last hundred years, they had withered away. They were small and completely unusable, like a pair of old dark green towels drying out.

He wore no armour, as it was most comfortable that way. He liked to feel the gold against his bare body when he rested in the morning. But of course, he liked it when he rested in the afternoon, evening, and certainly at night too. It was cozy to sleep, and inside his cave, it was always quiet and peaceful.

"Thud, creak, kadang," now echoed in his hall.

The strange clomping was not something one could sleep through, no matter how content.

The dragon awoke and quickly sat up, his glowing eyes scanning the hall for intruders. Art's jaws were open, ready to instantly spew fire at unwelcome visitors.

Thieves, he thought, someone is trying to steal my gold.

It turned out not at all difficult for the dragon to spot the knight, who, oblivious to the danger, tramped on and was heading straight for him.

The dragon began to speak aloud, a habit he had started after the first ten years of solitude.
"Well, what is this? A warrior in my treasure chamber, how did you get in?" the dragon muttered, quickly checking to see if there were any more new guests in the hall.
All seemed calm; he could see no more intruders.
The dragon tilted his head and looked with a smile at the clumsy armour that, with wobbly steps, made its entrance into the chamber.
"What a fool," muttered Art. "Are you trying to steal my treasure? You won't live long, little tin metalhead."
With a few quick strides, he stood right in front of the intruder.
"Now I'm going to have a barbecue with you! Ha ha," he laughed.
He threw his head back, and when it hurled forward again, a wave of fire swept over the knight. A wave of heat filled the hall. The armour was glowing from the intense heat.
"Well, that's that, no one has ever survived my barbecues," said the dragon, licking his lips to cool them.

Chapter 2:

Thirty Minutes Earlier

Prince Robert Wenchester had to lift his feet over stones and gnarled roots on his journey up to Mount Dragon. He breathed heavily, not because he was nervous; he had planned everything carefully over the last few months, but it was the heavy armour that made him pant. He carried no weapons, but he had a rope slung over his shoulder.

It had gotten dark, and it was raining and blowing heavily. When he turned around, he could still see the lights from the village down in the valley. The people there had been helpful and friendly, but when it was time to go up to the mountain, that was the end of it; up there, he had to fend for himself.

The village was named Wyrmville, probably because it was so close to Mount Dragon, but the name might also originate from the annual dragon festival when everyone in the village flew kites and celebrated. The village lay in the middle of the large country of Floriiana, ruled by King Alberath, who lived in the southern part. The prince ruled in eastern Floriiana.

In Wyrmville, no one had ever met or seen the king, but now, with this brief visit, they had met the handsome prince.
It was probably no one in Wyrmville who believed that Prince Robert would manage what he had set out to do; a pat on the shoulder was what he had received. The people in the village had nothing to lose on his foolish endeavour, but they were happy to sell equipment and information. The dragon's presence was a small source of income for the village. The little community provided the dragon with food and drink, and those responsible for this absolutely did not want to be involved in the prince's affairs. From now on, he would receive no help; he was entirely alone on his trek towards the mountain.

The path glowed faintly in the darkness, winding its way between the trees, and ended at a huge wooden gate embedded in the mountain. Once there had been a road here, but the trees had long since taken over the driving lane.

He slowed his steps; sneaking was not an option in the heavy storm, but somehow it felt better to move cautiously. The rain hammered against the gate, making it impossible for whatever was inside to hear any of his movements.

The gate was rounded at the top, the surface completely smooth, with neither a keyhole nor a handle. The wooden door was attached to the mountain with heavy hinges

decorated with ornately carved snakes. Similar stone snakes followed the curved arch upwards. Above the gate sat a grinning dragon's head, roughly hewn in stone, the colour long gone, as was a piece of one of the fangs. The head now stared with an absent gaze out over the valley. Robert took a few steps back and looked up. The silhouette of Mount Dragon was sharply outlined against the lightning in the clouds.
He knew he would find a small opening further up the mountain, as he had been told. A long-sealed and well-hidden ventilation tunnel that led straight into the heart of the mountain. He had memorised a map of where the opening should be, but that was all he knew.

He rounded the gate and continued upward. There was no longer a path, so he felt his way in the dark. Every time lightning flashed, he tried to memorise the terrain to navigate more easily. The climb became steeper, and the wind grew stronger as he ascended the mountain. The trees thinned, and among the crevices in the mountain, only a few scraggly bushes struggled to survive. He reached a large rock slab, free from bushes and grass. The surface glistened, and the heavy rain bounced off the hard surface. A large menhir stood majestically in the middle, watching over the night.

Robert stopped at the stone; he was now near the mountain's highest point. He would now walk forty-four steps in the direction of the village. The light from the village was barely visible in the rain.

He counted and hoped the stride length was right, despite the cumbersome armour. At forty-four, he stopped and turned left. In the flash of lightning, he could see the large stone over his shoulder. On the other side of the valley, he should now see another mountain, called Witch Mountain, also with a menhir on top. Ninety steps towards the witch, and then he should be there.

Despite the darkness, Prince Robert cautiously continued. The ground was covered with lingonberry twigs, moss, and stone, making it almost impossible to find a well-hidden opening. It seemed like an impossible task in the night's darkness, but the storm's cover was the only way to carry out the project.

"Eighty-eight, eighty-nine, ninety – here!" He knelt down and dug with his gloves, hitting the ground with his hands, hoping to find something hard. He searched in circles, or at least what he thought were circles. The hard things he hit were just stones.

Then it happened, the sound of metal against metal; his iron glove had struck something other than stone. He began to clear away the stones surrounding the metal object. He pushed the soil aside, exposing a metal hatch. The rain helped to wash the surface clean.

A large metal ring was attached in the middle. He grabbed it and slid the hatch aside. A musty smell streamed towards him. Yet, the warm light felt welcoming.

The hole was square, forty by forty centimetres, and went almost straight down. He paused and listened; only the

musty smell came up from the shaft below, no sound was heard. The knight took out the rope he had around his shoulder and tied it to a tree near the opening. Slowly, with a firm grip on the rope, he backed down into the shaft. The gravel crunched against his breastplate, and he heard tiny stones rolling down ahead of him.
Would his discreet intrusion be revealed before he even made it inside?

He closed his eyes while slowly lowering himself with the rope. The unpleasant sound of metal, gravel, and stone sliced through the air as he gradually moved downward in the passage. The metal in his armour amplified the sound, and inside the helmet, the crunching was dreadful. Occasionally, he stopped and listened, but he couldn't hear any other sounds from the depths below him.

Suddenly, he felt his feet dangling in mid-air. In the faint light, he could see that there were a few meters left to the ground and that the rope he had brought was a bit too short.
He listened, but nothing was heard. He climbed down as far as he could on the rope. Now he was hanging freely in the air with only one meter left to the ground.

He waited, the light from a powerful lightning flash quickly found its way down the shaft and almost blinded him.
Robert released the rope at the same time as the thunderclap and let himself fall to the floor. He heard the

clatter of his armour and the rumble of the thunder echoing in the cave as he hurried behind a pillar. After the thunderclap came silence; it seemed as though he was still undetected. He could hear raindrops gently hitting the ground after finding their way down the shaft.

The passage curved gently to the right, and on that side, there were about ten stone pillars. Between the pillars, a faint warm glow emanated.

All was silent.

The knight turned around and peered cautiously between the pillars, now seeing the heart of the cavern. There in the middle lay the dragon, asleep atop a pile of gold coins, amidst diamonds, and other priceless treasures. The dragon looked like a large human as he lay there, on his back with his arms under his head. The dragon's slightly lighter belly shone just like the gold in the light from the torches placed around in a circle.

Thick stone pillars supported the roof of the cave, and in the back of the hall, a large cage hung. In the cage lay the princess, her back turned this way, appearing to sleep. The knight didn't pay much attention to this but instead intensely scanned the objects scattered among the gold coins.
There, near the cage, lay a small, inconspicuous wooden chest, half-buried in the gold.

With cautious movements and sneaking between the pillars, he tried to get as close as possible. He made sure to keep an eye on the dragon at all times.
The modest chest did not seem to belong in a treasure chamber, yet someone had valued it highly enough to place it among all the gold.
For the last stretch to the chest, the knight had to sneak without the protection of the pillars. He knew if the dragon awoke, his end would be near.
He crept closer.
The gold clinked under his feet as they slowly sank into the coins. Upon reaching the chest, he tried to silently lift the small box, but it proved impossible as it was half-buried in the coins. He examined the chest, which had no lock. He cautiously opened the lid.
Inside the chest, there were several bottles, nestled in straw, all with beautifully handwritten labels. One of the bottles was marked Animate; he paid no attention to the others.
The bottle was heavy despite its small size, and he held it tightly in his hand as he carefully closed the lid.
As he sneaked back to the columned passage, rapid breathing was heard from the cage above.
There, imprisoned and humiliated, stood the beautiful princess. With her hands tightly clenched around the bars and a look of terror in her eyes, she now followed the knight's activities.

She said nothing.

The knight began to sneak towards the long passage that led to the gate. He walked along the pillars, casting a worried glance at the dragon each time he passed an opening. Would the dragon wake up? The knight threw a terrified look towards the centre of the hall every time he passed a pillar. Upon reaching the gate, he stopped to catch his breath. The gate was as smooth on the inside as on the outside, with no handles or locks.

Torches burned on the wall, the floor was covered with debris, trash, and food scraps; a major cleaning was needed here. He cleared an area on the floor free from debris.
The prince was nervous, but still felt satisfied; so far, everything had gone as planned.
The next step was to take off his armour. Quietly and carefully, he removed it piece by piece.
The armour was laid on its back, neatly on the floor. The knight, now in his underwear, also removed his helmet and placed it in position. Prince Robert Wenchester was a handsome young man, with long light hair.

The armour on the ground now looked like a resting person. Robert removed the seal from the bottle and opened it. He tilted the bottle and carefully dripped its contents onto all the pieces of armour in front of him. The green drops were instantly absorbed as they landed on the metal, like water drops on a dry sponge.
The armour began to glow, tremble, and shake, as if coming to life.

Robert put down the bottle and sneaked back into the hall. As he disappeared around the corner, the armour started to move. It had come to life, it was alive. The armour slowly sat up and looked surprised at its arms and legs. It had no past, it had not experienced anything before, it could not remember anything. As if we were trying to remember where we were and what we were doing before we were born.
The metal pieces tried to stand but fell back onto their bottom. The armour tried to rise again and with unsteady movements got to its feet. It began to walk with wobbly steps in the only direction it could, straight into the heart of the cave, the dragons cave. The hollow armour functioned as a resonating box, making its steps echo in the hall.
These were its first steps in life, and they were heard, loud and clear.

"Clank, creak, clang," echoed in the cave. The armour thought it was almost a bit fun how much it clattered when it moved. It learned quickly and stomped even louder. Suddenly, the armour stood right in front of a huge winged terror lizard.
"Now I'm going to have a barbecue with you! Ha ha," the creature laughed, and from its wide-open mouth and large nostrils, a violent fire erupted. Had there been a living person in the armour, they would have met a very hot and instantaneous death. Now, the empty armour was thrown backward like a glove.

This was not a good start to life; the armour shook its head and checked that all parts were in place. It glowed, but all the plates were where they should be. It realised this was not good, it had to stay away from the fire-breathing creature. The armour might be empty, but it was not stupid.

The dragon, on the other hand, felt satisfied having scored a direct hit, which usually sufficed to eliminate unwelcome visitors.

"He he, that takes care of that intruder. No one has ever survived a grilling from me."

The smoke cleared. But something wasn't right.

"But where did the intruder go?" muttered the dragon.

"Impossible, he can't just vanish into thin air like that!" shouted Art, looking around in every direction, even up and down.

Amidst the chaos, Prince Robert Wenchester, still in his underwear, rushed to the princess. He untied the rope from the cage and quickly lowered it so that it shattered. He helped the princess out of the destroyed prison. Prince Robert took her hand and ran to the rope he had used to enter.

Unfortunately, the rope was too high up, they would never be able to reach it.

They hid in a niche and waited.

The newly grilled armour stared around in surprise.

"What's happening? There's nowhere I can go, and all the while I'm being chased by a gigantic blowtorch," it thought as it quickly hid behind a pillar. The angry dragon quickly found it, and the fire flared so intensely that it was almost impossible to see anything.
The dragon charged wildly after the armour, hitting several pillars with its tail, causing many to collapse. The armour took another leap to the next pillar, and the dragon followed, spewing cascades of fire and hurling itself against the pillars, which collapsed. Never had the dragon needed to rush around like this to annihilate an intruder.

Prince Robert and the princess watched from a distance the wild battle between the dragon and the empty armour. The battlefield was now approaching their hiding place. A terrified suit of armour hurled itself towards them, landing right below the rope.
With a quick step onto the armour's back, Robert and the princess were able to grab the rope and climb up. They just managed to pull their feet in before a cascade of fire filled the passage below them. They crawled up through the air shaft with the help of the rope.

The ceiling of the cave now began to give way. Several pillars had been smashed in the frenzied chase. Stones fell from the cave's ceiling, and the armour sought refuge in a small alcove in the inner part of the cave. The dragon, intent on killing what he believed to be a burglar, paid no heed to the collapsing cave. He lashed out wildly and blew fire everywhere, determined to eliminate the intruder.

Now so much stone was falling that the armour feared the entire world was collapsing. Large boulders fell around him as he ran, with fire at his heels, into the tunnel where he was born.

The dragon followed, and just as the armour reached the passage towards the gate, the entire cave collapsed behind him. The massive gates of the exit came loose from their hinges and fell outward. The armour managed to jump out into the open with ease.

Feeling more like a birth than the awakening he had recently experienced in the dark cave, the armour contemplated the situation. The dragon, unable to follow, was trapped inside. The armour turned and saw that a large boulder lay across the dragon's back, rendering him completely immobile. With a helpless and terrified look, the dragon stretched a small arm towards the armour standing outside.

"Help me. Please, help, I'm stuck!" the dragon whimpered. "I'll die, please, help me."

The armour wasn't quite sure what to do. He was only a few minutes old. Nearly his entire short life had been spent being chased by the dragon, and now this unpleasant creature was asking him for help. Should he run away and leave the dragon to his fate? Where would he go?

He knew nothing about the world he had just entered. The dragon, after all, had chased him and tried to kill him, but why? Why had he, a suit of armour, appeared in a dragon's cave? He couldn't remember anything from before.
The dragon could surely answer many of his questions. He couldn't just leave the dragon to die; it felt wrong. When the large dragon's skull that sat above the gate suddenly fell down and shattered beside him, he made up his mind. He ran back in to try to free the dragon.

Now he was determined to save him.

He grabbed the dragon's outstretched hand and pulled. Stones tumbled around them. The armour tried to lift the large boulder lying across the dragon's back. In his eagerness, he knocked over a glass bottle with some liquid in it, but he didn't notice it. The armour took hold of the large stone with both arms and lifted with all his might. The block slowly lifted, and the dragon managed to free a leg and helped to lift. He could now crawl out.

They ran into the darkness as the dust from the total collapse of the cave washed over them.

Chapter 3:

Naming the Armour

Art turned around and stretched out his arms in despair.
"What happened? All my treasure is gone. How did this happen?"
Desperately, he looked up at the ruined gate.
"I have been collecting treasures for hundreds of years. Now everything is gone! Sigh!"
He sat down and tried to hide his face in his hands, but his face was much larger than his small hands. The dragon sighed heavily, not knowing what to do next. Just a little while ago, he had been sleeping soundly on his hoard. Now everything was gone, and the princess, was she left inside? He understood nothing of what had happened. Lightning flashed, thunder roared, and it rained, all at once. The armour stood beside the dragon. He knew nothing about anything. All he knew was that he had recently saved a dragon from certain death. He felt a certain security in the dragon. Now that his birthplace had collapsed, the dragon was the only thing he knew on this earth.

Art looked up at the armour.

"Thanks to you, my entire treasury is destroyed," he said, but at the same time, he realised that the knight had actually saved his life.
"Thanks for saving my life, too bad for you that you couldn't get to the treasure," the dragon assumed that this was a simple thief after his treasure.
The armour just stood still and looked.
"Go now, go home!" said Art.
The armour remained still; he had no home that he knew of.
"You have done what you came here for, you failed, return to your family," the dragon insisted. "There are no valuables left to steal."

But nothing happened; the armour did not move.
"Why are you just standing there, why don't you say anything?"
Now the armour started to feel a bit worried; the dragon seemed to be getting angry at him again. Was the dragon going to chase him once more? The armour, unable to speak due to the complete absence of vocal cords, shrugged his shoulders.
"What kind of answer is that? Who are you, really?" roared Art, now very irritated. The armour looked worried, scratched his temple, and appeared to be really thinking about it. Art had now stood up in front of the armour.
"Spit it out! Say something!"

The armour shrugged his shoulders again, he had given up, no matter how much he thought, he couldn't figure out what to do.
Art couldn't help but nag.
"You don't know?! Have you taken a blow to the head or something?" The armour shook his head. Now he could respond, and it felt better even though it was a negative answer. Art also calmed down a bit from the response.
"Show your face, and I will thank you once again for saving my life."
The armour then grabbed the hood of his helmet with both hands and lifted off the helmet and visor.
Between the shoulders gaped a hole; the armour was empty.
"You are... empty?"
Art's jaw dropped as he now understood how the armour had withstood his flames.
"Where did you come from?" The dragon realised as he said this that he would probably receive the same answer as before.
The armour put on his helmet again and pointed, somewhat surprised, towards the collapsed cave entrance.
"Yes, yes, but before that?"
The armour just looked sad; he couldn't answer. He didn't know; he knew nothing.
"You know nothing more than that you came from my cave?" asked Art.
The armour now nodded happily. He could answer, and that with a nod. It felt like he had done something good.

"I don't remember having any empty armour in my cave," pondered the dragon to himself.

The armour began to demonstrate the first moments he remembered. He first lay down on his back. Then he knelt next to it and gestured with his arms that the armour remained lying down. He showed how someone poured something over the armour. That person then put down a bottle and sneaked away. The armour quickly lay down again and demonstrated how he woke up and how he, with wobbly legs, continued into the cave. The armour was about to show how the dragon began to roar when Art interrupted the entire pantomime.
"Aha, it must be one of the magic potions that made you come to life. I always wondered if they really would work."

He looked at the armour. A small emblem was in the middle of the chest. A red Heart with a white flying bird. Art thought he had seen it before but didn't dwell on it.
"It was to deceive me, then the person went in and saved the princess," continued Art. He had noticed that the cage was broken and empty during the commotion but hadn't had the time to worry about it then. It felt good, that the princess probably wasn't left among the rubble.

The one who rescued the princess is probably far away now. Art thought that perhaps it was for the best; it might have been cruel to keep her in the cage. He now realised

that she did not enjoy life in the cave and hadn't been particularly fond of him either.
"She was too good at chess as well, I always lost," Art noted.

He quickly jumped to his feet again and looked up at the cave, or rather, the remnants of it. He sighed again, now he had nothing left.
He turned and looked at the armour standing beside him.
"Well then. I've got a friend, a knight friend," he said cheerfully. "Knight and knight, of course, you're just an empty suit of armour, but I like you."
"You must have a name, I'll call you Notalot, Sir Notalot, Sir Tom Notalot," said the dragon.
"I myself am Artemisia Dracunculus, but I am called Art." Art pronounced the long name slowly, but didn't think Tom would remember it anyway.
"I have no idea what we should do now, but we can't sit here in the rain all night."

They went back to the collapsed cave entrance, where the dust cloud had settled, now mixed with rain on the ground around them. They stepped over the ruined gate and tried to look into the cave. Everything appeared to be demolished. Some debris lay at the opening, and Art went forward to pick through the items, things that could be useful: a rope, a pot, and a sack.
"This could be useful while we live out in the open," he said, removing Tom's head and placing the items inside the armour. The pot settled sideways in Tom's "stomach",

with the rope and sack also fitting inside. For Sir Notalot, it felt good to have some 'innards.'

Art tried to crawl further into the cave to see if there were any small gold coins left, but just as he put his head in, the remaining small passage collapsed. There was nothing more of value to be found here.
Neither of the two noticed the faint green shimmer that covered the entire mountain.

Chapter 4:

Wyrmville

Dawn was breaking, the storm had moved on, the sun was on its rise, peeking curiously through the trees. They followed the path down the mountain for a bit, inhaling the fresh morning air. Art was amazed at how beautiful everything looked in the sunlight. He had only been outside the cave a few times in recent years, and then only at night.

Sir Notalot was fascinated by everything, the small drop falling from the leaf, the bark on the trunks, he stared directly into the sun and couldn't decide what was most fantastic. He felt a vibration in his feet. The ground shook slightly as if there was a minor earthquake. Art and Tom stopped; it must have been another collapse in the cave. Art turned around but could no longer see the opening of the cave.

"Come on, let's move on," said Art, patting Sir Tom on the shoulder.

The trees thinned out, the ground levelled off and they walked out onto an open field with short grass.

They were approaching Wyrmville and the field was one of the many pastures that surrounded the village. The dragon knew he was not so well-liked among the people who lived there. "We're nearing the village, best we don't

go too close," said the dragon and added, "I think it's better for us to take a different route."
They veered towards the edge of the forest that bordered the field. Tom thought it was a wise suggestion and looked appreciatively at the dragon. Art saw it and chuckled to himself. For the first time, Art had someone who liked him. Someone who relied on him. He didn't want the armour to see the people's reaction if they entered the village. A dragon that grills everything and kidnaps princesses doesn't become particularly popular. The dragon paid the village for their food and service, but they disliked him, and if they saw him outside the cave, they would be very frightened, Art knew.
"They are not so nice there, just ordinary people."
From a distance, they could see some women harvesting vegetables in the field. The children played nearby. Everything looked calm and peaceful.
Sir Notalot looked in wonder at the people. They seemed kind in a way, and he also noticed that they had the same body shape as himself. He smiled when he saw the children playing. Tom wanted to go there, he wanted to join in and laugh.
Then suddenly two black creatures came out of the forest, they looked like terror lizards as they rushed across the field. Their powerful hind legs gave high speed, the smaller clawed forelimbs were held tight against the body. Their terrible screams cut to the core and echoed over the valley. They moved quickly, like horses in full gallop. Their large jaws chewed and their long tails whipped in the air. The women quickly gathered the children and ran

towards the village. They were almost at one of the houses when one of the women lagged behind. She was quickly attacked and pulled down. The other creature rushed over. They stood on the woman's body and threw their heads back and forth, producing a chilling cry, a kind of victory scream. Then they began to bite and tear at the body.
"Come," shouted Art to Tom. "We must save her."
They rushed as fast as they could across the field. The dragon had great confidence in his powers and believed he could very well save the woman.

As they were almost upon them, both lizards looked up. They had no fur, their skin was matte black, like dried blood. Their eyes glowed faintly red. The jaws drooled, and blood splattered as they shook their heads to scream. Seeing the dragon and the armour, they dropped their prey and quickly ran away in opposite directions.

Art and Tom stopped, puzzled and unsure whom to chase. They heard screams and shouts from the other side of the house. Suddenly, the villagers came around the corner, with pitchforks and scythes raised high.
"There they are!" they shouted, rushing towards the dragon and the armour.
Art looked down at the wounded woman; she was bleeding heavily but was alive. He didn't know what to do. One thing was clear, they couldn't stay and explain. He turned around, grabbed Tom, and shouted at him.
"Run!"

They ran across the field, aiming for the forest which now seemed much further away than just a moment ago. A strong man at the front threw a scythe at them. It rotated through the air in a wide arc before landing with its blade straight into the ground next to Art's foot.

Some of the men had stayed to help the woman on the ground, but most had continued and were rushing full speed across the field, after Art and his friend.
Art's condition wasn't great, having rested on his gold hoard for the last hundred years had made him almost a bit stiff. Yet, with his strong and long legs, he could maintain a good speed.
Tom was a bit unaccustomed to running but managed to keep on his feet. The villagers were not used to running either and couldn't close the gap on them. Art and Tom reached the forest, leaped over a small ditch, and continued to rush forward.

They ran for many hours. Occasionally, they stopped and could hear in the distance that the villagers were still after them. They looked back but couldn't see anything because of the trees. Art moved aside to get a better view, but new trees constantly appeared, obscuring his sight. They kept running. It wasn't until the afternoon that it quieted down behind them, and they could slow down. The villagers had probably tired and turned back home.
"What happened? What were those creatures we saw?"
Art began to sense trouble. He had encountered these creatures before, long ago, several hundred years earlier.

They came from the underworld and were hideous creatures. They were called cabras, and they were abominable terror lizards, killing everything in their path. A long time ago, an earthquake created a crack down to the underworld. All manner of vile creatures crawled out and spread terror and destruction across all of Floriiana. There was war on all fronts, and the unrest lasted for many years. That time, everyone had helped each other, dragons, giants, humans, and the dwarf folk. All united and managed to kill many cabras over the years.
"We then gathered the remaining herd, drove all the cabras back into the underworld, and sealed the rift," the dragon concluded.
"The lizards we saw today were cabras, I know that now," said the dragon firmly.

Art and Sir Notalot wandered through forests and valleys, spending the night sometimes in a cave if they found one, and occasionally sleeping under the open sky.
The dragon actually wanted to go back and destroy those two cabras. But he realised that he and the armour would only meet trouble if they showed up near the village again. It was best to leave it be; they could do nothing.
Moreover, Art realised that he could no longer breathe fire. His wealth was what enabled him to breathe fire. Now, without his riches, he was devoid of his fiery breath.
All affluent dragons could breathe fire and spread death and destruction around them.
They had no specific destination in their wanderings. Art was enjoying his new life; he felt free in some way, a new

way of living. In the past, when he had all his gold, he believed he was free to do whatever he wanted, for being rich means having the means to do whatever one wishes. But since he was always guarding his treasure, he couldn't really do anything at all. He left his treasure chamber sometimes, but immediately became anxious that something might be stolen or destroyed during his absence.
Art now realised that he had been a prisoner in his cave for a hundred years, very wealthy, but still a prisoner. He began to understand that he had lived a poor life.

During their journey, they avoided roads and other major trails. Although they seldom encountered people, it was still best to stay away. They often found smaller paths leading to houses or farms. When nearing a settlement, they would take a detour around it. Art often found edible things near the settlements, like some discarded potatoes, perhaps some carrots, and sometimes Tom sneaked among the chickens to pick eggs for his dragon friend. Usually, there was a small path on the other side of the settlement, so they could continue their journey.

Art frequently pondered what they should do, where they should go. He had no friends, he didn't know any other dragons, he was probably the last dragon. The last time he saw dragons was during the war against the creatures from the underworld, a hundred years ago. He didn't know what had happened to them, as he had only cared about himself and his treasure.

They wandered for three days, constantly heading southwest, through a strange landscape consisting of forest, meadow, and again forest. Art hadn't been in this part of the country for many years. He didn't know much about this part of the world. Perhaps that was why he had chosen that direction, to have something completely new to start with. Often when one is about to start something new, it's just as well to start afresh.

That day, they had walked far and were both very tired when darkness fell. They had just crossed a small stream and then climbed up a small hill, a good place to camp. The forest had thinned, and had it been a bit lighter, they would have had a fine view over the landscape.
Art thought they should stop and sleep under the open sky. He liked having only the sky above him when he slept. The sky was exciting to fall asleep to; it changed a little each evening. The dragon thought about the ceiling of his cave, how he sometimes seemed to have seen the stalactites grow. The sky made him feel extra free in some way, he couldn't explain how. It was also a starry night, which was particularly beautiful.
Tom was so tired that he almost fell asleep standing, but then collapsed and landed with a thud on his back.
"I take that as a yes," said the dragon, looking towards the stream they had just passed.
"I'm going back to the creek for a drink."

The moon was not visible, but the stars twinkled in the bubbling water as Art lowered his large muzzle into the water. The cold water was fresh and delicious. Then he saw some other stars twinkling in the water. Red stars, in pairs.

Surrounded by twenty cabras, Art was in a perilous situation. They were not there to ask for directions. Art lunged to the side, attempting to escape, but was immediately attacked. Their tails whipped around like lashes and jaws snapped from all angles.

The dragon stood little chance; several cabras pounced on him, and he fell backward into the creek. Their jaws clamped onto his legs and arms. Dragons have tough skin, but this was too much. Instinctively, Art tried to breathe fire on his attackers. Not only he but also the cabras were surprised by the large flame that burst forth.

Art knew that his wealth had been the fuel for his fire, and now, being without riches, he shouldn't have had any flame. But there was no time to ponder this. The cabras closest to him lost their grip but were quickly back for more. One cabras leaped onto Art's neck. The fire had only stopped them momentarily. Now, unable to breathe and thus unable to breathe fire, Art was helpless. With a cabras around his neck and several others around his legs, he could do no more. He was running out of air and gradually losing all his strength.

Slowly, he sank into the cold water, a cabras clinging to each limb and one around his neck. This was the end.

Tom, awakened by a bright flash of light that was like lightning but without thunder, sensed something was amiss. Sitting up, he was surprised to find Art not beside him. Peering into the black night, he noticed the commotion near the creek. Standing up to get a better look, the darkness made it impossible to discern what was happening. Driven by curiosity, he began to sneak down the hill.
The splashing in the water and grunts were audible as he approached. Looking around, Tom couldn't spot Art anywhere and suspected that the dragon might have fallen into the creek.

Reaching the creek, Tom found a large number of cabras standing in a circle, partially in the water, partially on land. They were too engrossed in submerging something under the water to notice him. As one cabras leaped backward, running around the group before jumping back in, Tom caught a glimpse of someone lying in the middle of the turmoil. Sneaking closer, he saw Art lying motionless in the water, completely surrounded by cabras. Enraged, Tom charged forward recklessly, not caring about the number of cabras. No one was going to treat his best friend like this. He plunged into the water, causing a splash. Initially, it seemed like none of the cabras noticed him. Then, as if on a silent command, all the cabras turned towards the armour, released their hold, and fled screaming from the scene.

Tom rushed over and immediately pulled Art out of the water. The dragon was bleeding in several places, and Tom was uncertain about his fate. Art was breathing slowly, but otherwise, he was completely motionless.

Sir Notalot sat vigilantly through the night, watching over Art. He couldn't bear to lose his only and best friend. Art had been a constant presence in Tom's life for nearly as long as he could remember. The thought of anything happening to him had never crossed Tom's mind. To Tom, Art was as fundamental and indispensable as parents are to a child; it was unimaginable for them not to be there.

No cabras appeared that night.

In the morning, Art showed signs of recovery. He opened his eyes and saw Tom sitting beside him. The wound on his neck had stopped bleeding, and Tom had wiped away most of the clotted blood during the night.
"I was able to breathe fire when I was attacked," Art whispered. "I shouldn't have been able to, as my treasure was the fuel for my flame." He took a few heavy breaths, then continued,
"But it hardly helped."
He attempted a small laugh, but it caused him pain, resulting only in a slight shake.

Art lay by the creek for a long time, recuperating. By midday, he had recovered enough for them to continue their journey. Art wanted to leave the dreadful place where he had been attacked, seeking to put distance between them and the traumatic events of the previous night.

Art's thoughts were heavily occupied with the cabras. The first time they encountered them near Wyrmville, there were only two. This time, there had been twenty. If they were attacked again, they would stand no chance. It was peculiar how all of them suddenly fled at Tom's appearance. The armour didn't bear any weapons, nor did he attack; he simply made his presence known. This was very strange to Art.

On the other hand, Tom found the entire world to be puzzling, and he didn't ponder why the lizards were afraid of him. His perspective was different from Art's, perhaps due to his nature as a suit of armour or his lack of experience with such creatures. This contrast in their reactions highlighted the differences in their characters and experiences. While Art, a dragon with centuries of life and encounters, analysed and questioned their situation, Tom, new to the world in his form, accepted things more at face value, finding everything around him to be a wonder.

Chapter 5:

A Time for Questions

As they continued their journey, the landscape began to change. The forests grew sparser and less frequent. Days were spent walking through dry grasslands, with few communities or even farms in sight. In the distance, they spotted a herd of wild horses. For a moment, Art mistook them for cabras, but he relaxed when he heard their cheerful neighing.

Looking westward, they could make out snow-capped mountain peaks in the far distance, or were they just clouds? It was hard to tell; sometimes they seemed like mountain peaks, but the next moment they would morph into clouds. Regardless, that seemed to be their destination. They didn't know why, but Art felt changing direction now would render their previous journey pointless.

Their friendship was strengthening. However, they were unsure about what to do with their adventure. The dragon no longer wanted to guard treasures; being wealthy had become dull. Kidnapping princesses was not his thing either. He wanted to mentor the armour into being a fine piece of metal, feeling like a father to him. He wanted to do good, to be someone the armour could look up to. Maybe in this way, he could atone for his past misdeeds.

"I know what we should do!" he exclaimed one day as they trudged through the dry grass. "We shall rescue princesses in distress, those who are held captive." There was silence for a moment. The armour pondered and then nodded in agreement; it was a good idea.
"I've been a selfish dragon, only thinking about myself and my treasures. I now realise how foolish I've been, how silly it was to kidnap the princess. Wealth is a dangerous disease, one easily caught when hoarding treasures, leading to foolish actions," Art reflected. This newfound purpose set a different tone for their journey, one that was not only about discovery and survival but also redemption and doing good in the world.
They continued their silent journey.

Art knew that princesses were often held captive; he had once kept a princess in his cave. He had heard tales of princesses locked away in palaces, often confined to towers.
"But where can we find imprisoned princesses?" Art mused aloud after a while. The armour looked around as if expecting to find them nearby. Of course, an armour, unaware of much of the world, might not be the best to ask.
Art concluded that they needed to find a way to communicate with humans about the princesses. But how? A dragon was hardly the right individual to pose

such a question. He couldn't just walk into a village and inquire about a princess; he would be attacked immediately.
"And you, my dear armour, look like a human, but you cannot speak."

As they marched on, Art racked his brain for a solution on how to approach the humans. Tom also appeared to be deep in thought, but it was unclear what he was contemplating. Perhaps he was pondering the same issue, or maybe his thoughts were on something entirely different. The duo, each in their own way, was grappling with the challenge of how to embark on their new mission of rescuing princesses.

After a while, Art thought he had a good idea. He could be the voice for the armour, remaining hidden while making it appear as if the knight in armour was speaking.

Resolved to try this approach, they continued their journey but saw no communities or farms nearby. In the afternoon, they reached a forest, and at its edge ran a country road crossing their path. Judging by the tracks, it was quite frequented, with signs of carts and other traffic. Deciding it was as good a place as any to wait rather than choosing a direction at random, they prepared for their little act.

They walked along the road until they found a tree with a broad trunk close to the road, an ideal spot for their

performance. Tom positioned himself against the tree, while Art stepped out onto the road to survey the stage. Despite the somewhat unusual sight of a fully armoured knight leaning against a tree in the middle of nowhere, Art felt it looked natural enough.
"Does it feel okay?" Art asked, and Tom nodded in affirmation. Art squeezed behind the tree, initially dismissing Tom's observation that parts of him were visible from the sides. Eventually, Art had to concede and suck in his stomach. Neither of them wanted to find a bigger tree, especially since this was the widest tree Art had ever seen.

Now, they were ready to meet people, with Art discreetly hidden and ready to voice for Tom. The anticipation of their first interaction under this new guise was palpable.

They waited.

After a while, they heard heavy steps and soon after, they saw a traveler coming down the road. His long cloak was beige with dust. The man walked slowly, his gaze fixed only a few meters ahead of him. At first, the man did not notice the armour

standing by the side of the road. Perhaps it was his bushy eyebrows or his wide-brimmed hat that impaired his vision. It could also be that Tom was hard to spot; he simply did not exude a presence, which was quite understandable.

As the man came alongside the armour, Art began to speak. He had snatched Tom's glove, holding it over his mouth to sound as if he was speaking from inside the armour.

"Excuse me, sir, could you help me with a small question?" The old man stopped, looked up, and examined the knight. There were many impressions for him to process, and it took some time, but after a moment's thought, he replied.

"Sure, if you tell me who you are and can explain what happened to your left hand."

Tom looked down at his arm in surprise. Where his glove should have been was now just an empty space.

"I can do that," answered Art from behind the tree. "I am Sir Notalot and I am searching for imprisoned princesses, as I rescue princesses in distress."

Tom felt proud and straightened up; it felt good when Art said such positive things. Praise does well, even if one is an empty suit of armour. Praise is like frying in butter.

"Rescuing princesses is my specialty," Art continued. "I lost my hand in a battle with a splendid and beautiful dragon. Nonetheless, I managed to save the princess."

The man looked down at his own attire.

"I am no princess and I am not in any more distress than I can handle myself," the man replied.

"I mean, have you heard of any princess nearby, someone who is in distress and needs rescuing?"

"Hmm," the man took a long moment to think. "I believe I actually have heard of a princess," he said, glancing backward over his shoulder as if the direction would help jog his memory.
"She was held captive by an ugly and stupid dragon at Mount Dragon, many days' journey to the northeast." He pointed in the very direction from which Art and Tom had come.
"But she was recently rescued by a handsome prince."
Recognising himself as the 'ugly and stupid' one being referred to, the dragon felt a surge of irritation towards the old man.
"I've heard that it was actually a very beautiful and intelligent dragon," Art interjected, aiming to alter the narrative.
"Not at all," the man countered firmly. "There was a village nearby, and all its inhabitants agreed that he was arrogant and dreadful."
Now Art became very irritated and roared into the glove.
"Terrible can be yourself!"
He was so angry that a small flame ignited in his mouth.
At that moment, Tom turned around, walked around the tree, took back the glove, and smacked the dragon on the head with it.
The man was startled, not by the sight of someone being hit with a glove, as he had seen that before, but the sight of a living dragon was something he had never witnessed.
The man hurriedly continued on his way, now with a more vigilant gaze and significantly quicker steps than before.

The dragon was greatly startled by the blow he had received.
"Why did you do that?" he roared.
He placed his hand on his forehead as if trying to prevent the rapidly growing bump from getting larger. Tom just shook his head; he had nothing to say. The dragon quickly calmed down.
"Sorry, it was foolish of me to get angry at that man."
The dragon quickly understood what Tom had meant by striking him, realising it was unnecessary to act the way he had. Art recognised that they would never find any princesses if he continued to behave so foolishly.

Tom felt almost a twinge of regret for having struck so hard when he heard the dragon's remorseful tone. To lighten the mood, he playfully pretended to roar into the empty glove before handing it back to the dragon.

Sit Notalot then resumed his position in front of the tree, with Art behind it. They were once again ready for new travelers.

They waited.

A little later, a cart pulled by an ox approached. The load was covered with a large beige cloth. On the driver's seat sat a man, half asleep. He wore billowy green trousers and a thick sweater. Upon seeing the armour, he woke up and looked around nervously. Were there more knights nearby? Bandits usually didn't wear armour, did they?

Could it be a newly established toll, a border guard? The man was a trader and thought that he might now have to start paying a toll on his goods. This was not good; he preferred that they didn't inspect his cargo, but if he were stopped, he would be positive and helpful, as such misfortunes usually resolved well.

He let the ox continue at the same pace as before. The man looked at his feet, hoping the guard wouldn't bother him. He held both thumbs and reins as he passed.
Then a muffled, tinny voice was heard. "Excuse me, my noble sir, could you help me with a small question?"
"Of course," the man replied, quickly realising that it was wise to be accommodating. "Hop on, let's hear it.
Good, no order to stop. The man didn't slow the ox, it shouldn't be a problem to climb on at the slow pace. Tom hesitated but realised he couldn't just stand there. He jumped up and sat next to the man.
"What was it you wanted?" the man asked, looking a bit astonished at Tom. He probably found it strange to see someone in full battle gear in the wilderness, during peacetime, with helmet, visor, and all. Not all his peppers were green, he thought. He also noticed that the knight was missing a hand. There was no weapon or shield either. A very peculiar knight, the man summed up.
"My name is Gandhini, who are you?" he said. Silence followed for a while. He thought perhaps the man in armour didn't catch the question.
"I'm on my way to Larchville with my goods," the man continued. "It's not much in the way of goods, really," he

quickly added, not wanting his load to seem valuable. Wanting to change the subject, he asked.
"What was your question again?"
Tom realised that there wasn't much he could do at the moment. He chose to remain seated, perhaps out of politeness or maybe because everything seemed a bit exciting. For him, this was one of the first humans he had encountered. Tom found the man to be pleasant, noting that they shared a similar body form. Tom wished he wasn't mute, that he could talk to the man.
Gandhini was relieved that the man in armour was neither a robber nor behaving like a customs officer. It was nice to have company, and he began to briefly talk about where he was headed. It was nice to have someone who listened, and he thought his new passenger might start talking eventually.

But that never happened.

Tom and Gandhini continued sitting quietly on the wagon, moving along. Sometimes it can be quite comfortable just to sit in silence. At that moment, both felt it was one of those times.
Eventually, Gandhini couldn't hold back any longer.
"I'm so eager to hear your question. What did you need?"
Tom scratched his helmet and didn't notice the beasts that leaped out on each side of the wagon. Two cabras charged and attacked the ox. One grabbed a large bite over its head, while the other jumped onto its back. Gandhini reached for his knife, which he had on the flatbed.

Tom stood up. Out of pure reflex, he made the same movement he had done the last time when he scared away these beasts. He raised his arms to appear as large as possible. Believe it or not, it worked. The beasts paused and looked up at the armour standing on the driver's seat with arms outstretched. They immediately let go of the ox and fled in opposite directions. The animals disappeared into the forest, and then all was quiet.
Gandhini just stared at Sir Notalot, unable to comprehend how this had happened. He hadn't even managed to draw his knife. Gandhini realised that had the knight not been on the wagon, he would have had to deal with these beasts himself, and it wouldn't have been easy. He would have undoubtedly lost his ox, and perhaps his own life. Now the ox seemed unharmed, and he was just a bit shocked.

Now Tom wanted to get off and go back to Art. He leaned forward slightly to indicate that he was about to get off. Gandhini wanted to give something as a thank you to his mute saviour and insisted that he sit down again. The man reached under the cloth on the flatbed and pulled out a small box. Inside were small brown glass bottles wrapped in cloth. Gandhini took out a bottle, carefully unwrapped it, and looked at the label for a moment before handing it to Tom.
"Take this as a thank you for saving me and my ox," he said.
Tom accepted the gift. On the handwritten label was just one word, *speak*.

Tom hopped off the wagon and bowed politely. He stood still, watching as the wagon slowly rolled away. He looked at the bottle for a while before tucking it inside his armour.

Art was waiting by the roadside when the armour came trudging back. He scolded Tom at first. He was actually angry. To just sit and ride off like that with a stranger. It was evident from Art's demeanour that he had been worried. After a while, he calmed down; everything had gone well, after all. They both agreed that they would ask more people, but Tom would not ride along even if the people asked him to.

They waited.

A man came walking from the north. He was strongly built and walked briskly. He was bearded, wearing robust clothes and a large backpack. He looked like a real long-distance walker.

The man gave such an impression that Tom was almost a bit frightened. Even though Tom looked hesitant, there was no doubt in his voice.

"Excuse me, sir, do you have a moment to help me with a small matter?"

The man stopped and looked at Tom.

"Who are you?" the man wondered.

"My name is Sir Notalot, and I come from a place called Wyrmville," said Art from behind the tree, and continued. "Where are you from?"

"My name is Draven. I come from Singua, a city in Faroon, far to the west."
"Interesting," replied Art. "I am actually on my way west."
"It's a difficult journey. It's a trip I definitely wouldn't recommend," responded Draven, shaking his head. Art disregarded the advice and continued with his questions.
"I'm looking for imprisoned princesses, as I rescue princesses in distress. Do you know of any in distress in the Western lands or nearby?"
"No, no princesses," said Draven, looking up at the mountain range. "It's a wealthy land with many castles and large estates. I encountered many soldiers, but they were hunting dragons, not princesses."
"Are there dragons in the west?" Art could hardly hide his excitement. Luckily for him, he was behind a tree, otherwise, he might have hugged the man. This was more than he had hoped for. He had long believed he was the last dragon.
"They were searching for dragons, but I doubt their existence," the man said. "Fairy tales aren't my belief."
Sir Notalot thought it was best to end the conversation. The latest answer gave him the feeling that this discussion too could end badly. He took a step back and bowed as a thank you. Art was somewhat speechless by the comment and didn't manage to say anything before the man began to walk away, adding, "Thank you."

He continued along the path and quite quickly, Art emerged from his hiding place. He wanted to talk with

Tom about what had happened. Of course, he couldn't actually talk to Tom, but he wanted him in front of him as he thought about the possibility of other dragons and what that could mean. What they didn't see was that someone in the man's backpack was spying on them. The figure watched them for a long time before jumping out of the backpack and slipping down into the ditch.

***

A powerful storm sweeps across Mount Dragon. Rain and lightning lash out, water violently strikes against stones and tree trunks. The wind tears at the tree branches and rips through the low clouds rushing across the sky. The door to the dragon's chamber lies shattered on the ground. The cave has collapsed, but the strong wind still manages to find its way into the mountain. Inside, a bottle rolls due to the draft, its contents having spilled and mixed with the rubble.

The broken walls begin to slowly move, in and out, as if they were breathing. Outside in the rain, on the mountain's sides, a pair of deeply set eyes open. The dark eyes look around in surprise, searching in the darkness for something to fixate on. The eyes then spot a dragon and a man in armour walking down the slope.

The breathing becomes more intense. The mountain lies still, as if gathering strength. Then the ground starts to shake like an earthquake. Several elongated cracks open along the sides. Trees begin to topple on the slopes. The entire mountain sways, back and forth. The cracks widen further and with immense willpower, the entire mountain stretches itself and with a jerk, tears away from the bedrock. The eyes gaze out over the landscape, a landscape that has been there for hundreds of thousands of years, but which the mountain has never before seen. Then the mountain begins to slowly move down the slope. A large crater opens up where the mountain previously stood. Water flows down towards the bottom, where a hole opens, and the accumulated water continues down into the underworld. From the dark hole, yellow-green gas streams out, mixed with roars and terrible screams. Suddenly, a terrifying creature emerges from the hole, sniffing the darkness, tasting the night. It is a cabras, and more of them follow. The beasts chew the air as they slowly climb up towards the edge. Their large red eyes faintly glow in the night. Huge hands emerge from the hole, breaking apart the edge to widen it. Dirty mountain trolls then crawl up and roar at the creatures to stick together. The long whip they hold in their hands whistles through the air, a necessity to control the filthy and hideous beasts.

"Death to the dragons!" they bellow.

Chapter 6:

The Limberik

Art opened his eyes, he was out of breath, was it a nightmare? He sat up, despite the darkness he could see Tom sleeping soundly on the other side of the glowing fire, too close for Art's liking, but Tom seemed to find it comfortable. Art touched his forehead, closed his eyes, and wondered what kind of terrible dream he had had.
He felt the bump and remembered what had happened the day before. After all their encounters, they had left the road and continued towards the mountains. They still wanted to head west, and now that Art had heard rumours of dragons, it felt even more important to him.
Art added more wood to the fire but found it hard to fall back asleep, lying awake for a long time pondering dragons and demons.
It was early in the morning, the sun was about to cross the horizon. Its warm light was already reaching the highest peaks in the west, soon the whole plain would be bathed in sunlight. The fire had long since died out, and the ground around was damp from the cold night. Art had fallen back asleep, and Tom was still in a deep slumber.
A very small person, just an arm's length in height, moved quickly around their camp. The tiny figure scrutinised the two sleepers, then hopped over the armour and squeezed through the visor of the helmet. Tom noticed nothing.

"It's quite spacious and comfortable in here, one could say," was heard from inside the armour.
It seemed as if Tom was speaking. "One could live here."
"Live, here?" Art wondered sleepily, without opening his eyes.
It was only after he had said this that Art reacted to what he had heard. He quickly sat up and stared in surprise at his companion. The sun had just reached them, and Art was dazzled by the gleam of the armour.
"You can talk?"
"Of course, I can talk!" was heard from inside the armour.
It was then that Tom truly woke up. Both the dragon and the armour looked at each other in astonishment. It was hard to say who was more amazed. But it probably had to be the armour, who also didn't understand what the discussion was about. It was only when a little face appeared behind the visor that they both understood what was happening. Someone was talking from inside the armour.
"Good ventilation too," said the little man, laughing.
"What sort of figure are you?" asked Art, thinking the little being was rather bold.
"Gecko is my name, we are often called Limberiks by the big people. I am a Limberik who has found a new and nice home."
The voice was now coming from a knee on the armour.
"Sometimes we are also called arm-length folk."
Gecko again stuck his head out through the visor.
"And who might you be?"

"My name is Art, a dragon who has lost his treasure, and not much of a dragon at that," replied Art but quickly wanted to know more about the little man. "Limberiks? Arm-length folk, I've never heard of them? Tell me more."

It's understandable that Art had never encountered these small people. They live in dark, damp caves, preferably those partially filled with water. Wet and dark is their preference. They are small and slender, skilled climbers. This peculiar race moves like lizards when they crawl on cave walls. Their eyes are large to see well in the dark. They are rarely seen during the day. But it's not that they despise light, it's more that daylight is harsh on their eyes. Their light, slightly moist skin is also not very resistant to sunlight. Therefore, they prefer to stay in their caves on the beautiful, sunny days when humans are out in the forest. They are known for their good humour, and Gecko might be the most jocular of all arm-lengths.
"Why isn't a dragon without its treasure much of a dragon?" wondered Gecko. "You look like a proper dragon to me."
"A big treasure gives me the power to breathe fire. Now I have nothing, except for a good friend made of metal," replied the dragon, sticking out his tongue to show a small flame on the tip.
"The only thing I'm good for now is lighting fires," he continued, sulking a bit.
"Okay, I won't tickle you there," came a voice from the armour's belly.

"What do you mean, tickle me?" wondered the dragon, not understanding. He hadn't been tickled anywhere.
"The tin man is a bit sensitive in certain places," said Gecko, looking out again. "I know because I can hear what the armour is thinking when I'm inside."
"That's peculiar," said Art. "What is this clanking suit of armour thinking then?"
"He says he likes the big frog."
"Oh, thank you. I like you too, I mean Tom, of course," Art replied somewhat hesitantly. "But I'm not a frog, I'm a dragon."

There was silence for a moment, as if the dragon couldn't think of anything to say now that he could talk to his best friend. Perhaps he was a bit puzzled that Tom had thought he was a big frog. Or maybe Gecko had made up the frog part. Just because you're green doesn't mean you're a frog, thought Art.
"I know of a castle where there might be princesses," shouted Gecko from inside the armour.
He had received a quick briefing from Tom about what had happened and what the two friends were out adventuring for.
"I know, because I passed by a big castle once. It had lots of towers and high walls."

Gecko quickly crawled out and now stood on Sir Notalot’s head, waving to illustrate the large castle. "I know where it is, I can show you," he said, pointing

straight west. "It's that way, but I think you have to head north to cross the river."
"We should be able to cross the river," Art replied confidently and wanted to take the most direct route.

They decided to go together to the castle Gecko knew of. After all, Art and Tom had failed in their attempts to find damsels in distress. If Gecko knew of a place, it was worth a try. The castle seemed to be in the direction they had been walking for the past few weeks. But it was far away, many days' journey, perhaps weeks. It had been a few years since Gecko was there, but he didn't think it would be difficult to find. They began their long journey immediately, and at the same time, the sun began its ascent in the sky.

Gecko preferred to stay in the armour because the sun was so strong. Over time, they became very good friends. For Art, it felt like he had gained two new friends because he could now talk to Tom almost like usual. Of course, he couldn't talk to Tom about Gecko. As it was now, Gecko acted as an interpreter.

After a couple of days of traveling west across the Perghoolas Plain, the knight and the dragon began to wonder how the tiny man had once covered this long distance. It must have taken several years for such a small person to walk so far. Considering that he could only travel at night, it was an incredible feat. Neither of them dared to ask, afraid that the little man would take offence, thinking they believed he had made it all up. They didn't want to hurt their newfound companion, but the farther they went, the more suspicious they became.

Chapter 7:

High Above the Ravine

In front of them was Granola, the enormous mountain range. It had long been on the horizon, and each day the mountains had slowly come closer. Now, they were at the Trip River, which marked the end of the plains, and the high mountains rose on the other side. The river flowed at the bottom of a ravine known as Dragonspine Ravine. The ravine was very wide and nearly a hundred meters deep. Trip River had its source far up in the icy north and then ran through this chasm all the way down to the sea in the south. There was a roaring sound as the river rushed among large stones down below. The chilly and moist fog drifted up in waves to the edge where the three of them sat, pondering how to cross.

"There should be a bridge," Art thought, but Gecko firmly replied that there was none. This made Art even more suspicious. "How did you cross then?" he wondered.

"I came from the north, where the river begins," answered Gecko. Art began to realise that they might have to take the long way. Not wanting to admit his mistake, he quickly replied.

"We have ropes. We can throw them across," suggested the dragon, but immediately realised the folly of his words. They would obviously need to be tied on the other side.

They began walking north along the ravine, as it seemed to narrow a bit further up. They also thought they saw something that resembled a bridge, or at least parts of a crossing.

But their joy came to an abrupt end. It turned out that this bridge had not been used for a long time, which was understandable. The middle section was gone. Two lone bridge pillars on each side were not much help. For a long time, the bridge was the only connection between Faroon in the west and Perghoola in the east. When it was destroyed during the war against the underworld, almost all exchange of information and trade between the countries ceased. North Gap remained, but it could only be crossed during the summer half of the year. Knowledge about each country faded into oblivion after the bridge collapsed. But the place they found should at least be the narrowest part of the ravine.
"We could probably throw you across," said Art, looking at Gecko, who looked back in horror.
"No, no, no, I'll kill myself on the other side."
He was willing to do a lot, but not to be thrown across a ravine.
"We'll fix a parachute, then you'll land softly," said the dragon reassuringly, showing with his hands how one lands with a parachute. The left index finger, representing Gecko, swung back and forth under Art's cupped right hand, representing a parachute. The dragon let the whole package land softly on the ground.

"But you can't throw me across with your small arms," Gecko shouted. He now stood up, gesturing wildly.
"I won't use my arms, I will sling you over with my tail," he said, approaching Tom.
He grasped Tom's upper body and detached it from the waist, quickly finding rope and fabric. He found the large sheet they sometimes used as a cover when it rained. He tied the ends under Gecko's arms. Then he brought out the rope and laid it in a ring at the edge of the ravine. Looking at the circle of rope, he concluded that this should work out fine. He picked up one end and weighed it in his hand.
"Hold on tight," he said to Gecko, as he placed the rope end in Gecko's small hands. Art folded the sheet into a ball and asked Gecko to sit down. The parachute package landed in Gecko's lap, who was then asked to curl up.
"When I shout, release the parachute, but keep hold of the rope, got it?"
"Hmm," answered Gecko, his face pressed into the sheet.
Art positioned himself a bit ahead and placed the end of his tail under the Gecko ball. Aiming for the other side, he needed to find the right height for the throw, and throw hard enough.
"Are you ready?" Art asked, pulling with all his might, and threw the package far out over the ravine. It was a strong throw, and the dragon spun so much that he almost went over the edge. Gecko flew gracefully, like a cannonball.
"Now!" Art shouted, having regained his balance and feeling it was time to deploy the parachute. But nothing happened; Gecko didn't react at all. The wind of speed

made it so he couldn't hear anything, and he didn't dare open his eyes. Limberiks like caves, dark and damp; flying is not their thing. He thought he was about to hit the ground soon. He waited for a shout from Art, but all he heard was the roaring of the wind. Deploy the parachute now, he thought and shouted loudly to himself. "Now!"

Just then, it was as if his body reacted and released the package with the fabric. "Flump," the sheet filled with air and jerked under his arms. Gecko held tightly onto the rope as he swung around and was left hanging in the air. He opened his eyes and saw the dragon and the armour hopping with excitement on the other side of the ravine. He didn't get to see much before he hit the ground. He rolled a bit before stopping himself by stretching out his legs. Everything had worked as planned.

Gecko tied his end of the rope around the largest of the bridge pillars and waited for Art to tighten the rope and tie it off on his side.

Once the rope was taut, Art stepped out and began his tightrope walk. It swayed and bounced, but it was no problem for the dragon. When he was a young dragon, he could fly and had therefore gained good balance and was not afraid of heights.

When Art made it across, he called to Sir Notalot to step out on the line. The armour quickly started out on the rope, which responded by swinging back and forth. Tom then went down on all fours and crawled. That didn't go so well either, and after a few meters, Tom was hanging upside down on the rope. This position didn't hinder Tom, who continued to crawl, and soon he too was across the ravine.

Tom felt it was a pity to leave the rope behind and wanted to go back to the other side to untie it. Art found it a bit comical that Tom hadn't thought about the consequences of untying the rope on the other side.
"Not this time," said Art jokingly. "Maybe another time."
Tom looked back at the rope for a long time as they began their journey towards the mountain range. He couldn't understand why he wasn't allowed to go back and retrieve the rope.

"Up here, there's a pass that allows us to cross over the mountain range," Gecko pointed out through his visor. "Last time I was here, I was in the pocket of a wandering man."
After a while, Gecko added another comment. "Just so you know and don't feel uncomfortable asking."
The dragon and the armour exchanged a slightly ashamed look. Tom realised that Gecko had heard his thoughts, his suspicions. The dragon also felt singled out and was somewhat embarrassed. So far, everything Gecko had told them had been true.

The mountain massif wasn't steep at first, but as the day progressed, the ascent became steeper and steeper. The rocky path twisted more and more the higher up they went. It was a tough hike for a dragon who had barely been outdoors in the last hundred years and for an armour that was only a few weeks old. The narrow pathway sometimes had steep cliffs on the side, and at times the path was completely gone, forcing them to climb. Tom saw snow for the first time.

On the evening of the second day, they reached the mountain ridge. Strong winds blew, and small white clouds cast their long shadows over the valley in front of them. It was cold. Everywhere they looked, there were forests, except for some parts that were too steep for trees to find a foothold. In places, clouds of water vapour rose from some of the many streams rushing through the forest. In the middle of the valley, they could discern a castle, but it was too far away for them to see any details. So far, Gecko's story held true.

They turned around and saw the ravine far below, the one they had crossed early the previous morning. They all felt that something did not seem right. Gecko was the first to comment.
"Look, was there really a mountain by the ravine where we crossed? Strange? I don't remember it looking like that."
Art became frightened, suddenly remembering his nightmare about a mountain that began to move. He did not want to believe it could be true. Could his dream somehow be real? He tried to convince himself it was

impossible and replied very irritably, as if his denial of what he saw would remove the mountain.
"Of course it was there, mountains can't just move and wander around. We didn't see it because we were so eager to get across the ravine."
Gecko, interested in discussing this fascinating topic, replied, "That's true, but actually, this armour shouldn't be able to..." He was quickly interrupted by Art.
"Enough talk about this, now we need to head down a bit before it gets dark."

They quickly found a sheltered spot to rest for the night. Art had trouble sleeping, his thoughts preoccupied with his nightmare. He didn't want to share his concerns with his companions. He too had seen the mountain by the ravine and couldn't remember it being there when they crossed the chasm. He just didn't want to think about it. Was this the mountain from his dream? Why was it following them? How could it possibly be moving? "No, I don't want to think about this at all," thought Art, pondering how the mountain could have crossed the ravine.

Art got up early and started walking down towards the valley, with the other two following, heading towards the forest. The trees grew larger as the forest denser. A small brook babbled beside the path.

After half a day's hike, the forest had become so dense that they could no longer see if they were going in the right direction. They followed the brook, which had now grown into a strong stream. Occasionally, they came to steep cliffs where the water hurled itself into the air with full force. Then, the group had to leave the brook for a while to find a passable way. However, it was seldom a problem to find their way back to the water, as it continued its loud, rushing journey down towards the valley floor.

Chapter 8:

The Castle in the Valley

On the second day, the armour was tired and had to ride on the dragon's back. Art kept talking as usual, and Gecko couldn't get a word in edgeways. They had started early that morning and everyone was in good spirits. Suddenly, Gecko heard something; he shushed to silence the dragon, but it was difficult. Tom understood and took a firm grip on the dragon's shoulders. Then Art realised he should be quiet.

Then all three heard a faint crying far away. The dragon immediately picked up the direction and rushed through the forest at full speed, with the armour on its back. It could be a princess in distress.

Unexpectedly, the forest ended and a steep cliff appeared in front of them. Art stopped suddenly, and Tom was thrown off, did a somersault in the air, and managed to grab hold of the dragon's large fangs at the last moment. There he hung. It was a very deep abyss. The dragon didn't care much about it; he was most impressed by the castle they had in front of them.

In the middle of the valley lay the most fantastic castle he had ever seen. Huge walls ran around the castle's many buildings. The castle had several towers of different heights, and some of the towers were connected by small

bridges. The largest towers had roofs of verdigris copper. Other towers were without roofs or had domes in red and green. Large red and yellow flags marked the towers' aspirations towards the sky. Art was just amazed. At the bottom of the ravine flowed a river that surrounded the large rock on which the entire castle area rested.
"Wonderful, fantastic. What a fantastic construction, the most beautiful I have ever seen."

He turned and twisted his head to take in all the towers and turrets, walls and gates. They could also hear that in one of the towers someone was crying, but it was too far away to see who or what it was.
"Listen, do you hear the princess who is imprisoned in the fantastic castle?" said Art. He couldn't stop being fascinated by this masterpiece of architecture, while the knight hung and swung in his two tusks.
"Look there, there is a path down to the bridge and the castle gates," continued the dragon eagerly. The narrow road down to the castle looked steep and perilous. It meandered like a serpentine with steep cliffs alternating on the left and right sides. In some places, there were small bridges along the path.

Tom could no longer hold his grip, the armour was heavy, the metal gloves began to slip, and it didn't get any better by the dragon tossing his head back and forth. He lost his grip. Gecko, who was afraid of heights, had crawled down into the right shoe. The armour fell, but the dragon, who was quick-witted in many ways, caught the armour over

his head. With a neat backward toss, he threw Tom back onto his back.
"Not so fast, Mr. Armour," said Art, looking back over his shoulder at Tom. "I think I know a better way. Not as quick, but much safer," he said and set off towards the castle with his two friends on his back.

He ran along the edge of the ravine to reach the road leading down into the valley. Sometimes he leaped, almost skipping. The dragon was in a good mood; after all, they were about to save the princess in the tower. He was convinced that they had finally found a princess in distress.

They reached the narrow trail leading down to the castle. The path turned out to be longer than they had thought, and it was also difficult to advance unseen. It was steep and arduous. There were steps that were sometimes high, sometimes long, and sometimes slanted the wrong way. They frequently stopped in the shelter of some rocks, constantly checking to ensure no one in the towers was spying on them. Art found it tough.
"Phew! That was a really tricky path."
"Ah! Slackers," Gecko muttered from behind the visor.

They still had a distance to go to the bridgehead when they again decided to stop and check the situation. From behind a rocky outcrop, they could see the bridge leading to the castle, ending with the castle's large gate. The bridge was narrow and long. There were no railings, just a

low row of stones to prevent carts from rolling over the edge. There was no place to hide on the bridge. They all looked worriedly towards the castle's entrance.
"It's going to be hard to reach the gate unseen," commented Gecko.
"But how are we going to get in? A dragon can hardly knock on the door and walk in saying good day, can it?" wondered Art. No one had a good answer. They decided to sneak up and take a look, then they could decide what to do next.
Suddenly, loud voices and the clatter of weapons were heard from inside the castle. Something was starting to happen inside. The dragon became even more anxious.
"Do you hear that? Something's happening in the courtyard." Something was underway inside; had they been discovered? They continued on and approached the bridgehead. They hadn't seen anyone in the towers spying on them. Everything seemed calm; no one should have seen them.

Just as Art set foot on the bridge, trumpet blasts and fanfares sounded. The enormous gates began to creak and slowly open. Thinking they were discovered, they rushed back to hide.
Unfortunately, there was nowhere to hide. Beside the road, there were only steep cliffs. They were forced to follow the road back. They ran as fast as they could up the hill. Art stopped and turned around to see an entire army marching after them. There was a standard-bearer at the front and behind him men with trumpets and drums, not

exactly what one sends out to stop intruders. Then came hordes of soldiers. The dragon and the armour hid behind a rock, but realised it was no protection. Once the soldiers reached them, they would be easy to spot. They had to run up, all the way up to the forest.

The armour and the dragon were thoroughly exhausted when they finally reached the forest. Tom sounded like a church organ, and Art was panting too. "I can't run anymore, let's hide here." They both threw themselves behind the nearest bush.

They waited and hoped the soldiers hadn't seen them; they couldn't muster the energy to move another step. They heard the sound of marching feet getting closer and cautiously peeked out from behind the bush.
First, they saw the standard, which was bright red with a golden, fire-breathing dragon. The standard-bearer, in his short skirt and metal breastplate, continued straight past them. Then came a brass band with yellow flags hanging under the long trumpets. A robust man was beating a large red drum.
All were dressed in red and yellow fabrics fluttering in the wind. The soldiers marched by in rows, all wearing metal helmets and red leather jackets. There were many soldiers; it seemed endless. Only after the entire troop had passed did Art dare to start talking again. Art was not often silent for such a long time and he sighed with relief, "Apparently, they were not after us."
He turned to Tom and Gecko. Both had fallen asleep.

Art woke them both and explained that they could now head down to the castle again. The two who had just woken up were not too keen on this, but Art explained that with a large part of the guard force on an excursion, the chances of being detected were small.

The steep path was just as strenuous as before, and the armour wished he would never have to walk this way again. They reached the gate without being detected and began to examine how to get in. Far below, they could see the dark waters of the river. The gate was locked and solid, not something that could be broken down in a jiffy.
"So, how on earth are we going to get in here?" wondered Art.
"I don't know," answered Gecko. "I might be able to sneak in somewhere, but I won't have the strength to open the gate for you once I'm inside."
"What do you say, Sir Notalot?" asked the dragon, looking at the armour. "How about getting into the castle?"
"He doesn't know. He doesn't like the physical training and is not thinking of running up the hill again!" said Gecko, but Tom was not done and added, "Then they might as well melt him down into a cast iron stove." Art could only agree.

They sat down on the bridge railing, pondering their next move when the gate slowly opened again. This time, there were no trumpets or fanfares. There was nowhere to run.

Art and Tom looked up in horror at the path while Gecko crawled even further into Tom's armour. It looked just as bad as the last time.
"As I said, I'm not running up the hill again either!" said the dragon, throwing himself over the bridge railing and grabbing the low stone railing. The armour threw himself after and grabbed the dragon. Holding onto a hanging dragon was not easy. He remembered when he held tightly onto the dragon's fangs and how his gloves slipped.
Indeed, this time the armour also slid slowly, this time along the dragon's back. When he grabbed the dragon's pitiful wings, they just folded up. He slid further out over the tail. Just when the armour thought it was over, he felt a stop. His feet had landed on the dragon's T-shaped tail. What luck that dragons have such tails.
"Phew!" sighed Gecko from inside the armour.

A guard stepped out onto the bridge and peered up the road. He was dressed similarly to the soldiers they had seen earlier, but he had some extra puffs on his shoulders and a long spear in one hand. The man seemed pleased that the entire troop had left, or perhaps he was just glad he hadn't had to accompany them.

Everything seemed calm for our adventurers, except that the stone the dragon had chosen to hang from had a small crack. A chip broke off under the weight, and the dragon was left hanging by one arm. The guard reacted immediately, lowered his spear, and walked towards the

edge. That's when Gecko decided to leave them. He crawled out of the helmet, up onto the dragon's head.
"I'm out of here!" he said and jumped up onto the bridge, starting to run towards the bridgehead.
"Blasted kids!" shouted the guard. "This is no playground. Scram!"

The guard pointed his spear after Gecko, who was hopping away up the road. Then, the guard stepped back through the gate and locked it behind him. He did not notice that the "child" was unusually small. Having not seen many children in his life, he didn't give it much thought.

Meanwhile, Art and Tom were still in a precarious position, with the dragon struggling to maintain its grip on the stone. They needed to act quickly and carefully to avoid detection and find a way into the castle. The situation was tense, but it also presented an opportunity. With the guard gone and most of the troops out, their chances of entering the castle unnoticed had increased. They had to make their move swiftly and wisely.

Chapter 9:

Chickens and crocodiles

The damaged stone had finally given way completely, breaking into a thousand pieces. Art, with the armour on his back, fell. The dragon instinctively tried to flap its small wings, but to no avail.

After what felt like an eternity, they both splashed into the rapid stream. The armour, being hollow, quickly floated to the surface, and the dragon grabbed onto it. The swift current and steep cliffs made it difficult to get to shore. Then Art noticed something startling: the stones along the banks seemed to be moving. They slithered down towards the water's edge and, with small splashes, disappeared into the water. The stones were getting closer to the bathing duo. When Art saw eyes poking above the surface, he realised they were crocodiles that had been lying on the rocks, waiting for suitable prey.

The crocodiles lived in the waters around the castle, waiting for animals and humans to fall in. It wasn't often that someone or something fell in, but crocodiles can survive a long time without food. The dragon knew how hungry one could be if it hadn't eaten in a couple of months. It was probably not the best idea to swim in these

waters. Things looked grim for both of them, but for the crocodiles, it seemed like a feast was imminent. One of the splashes was particularly heavy, suggesting there would be enough to share.
The first crocodile lunged, mouth agape, at the dragon, but Art managed to thrust the armour into its maw, thereby evading the initial attack. The second crocodile swam around and lunged at the dragon, but Tom managed to jam a leg into its jaw. The crocodiles had now only bitten into steel and, if crocodiles can make such determinations, realised this was not much of a meal. Iron-rich, perhaps, but not nutritious. They let go and swam back to the shore. Better luck next month.

Once again, the dragon and the armour were floating along the stream. The armour began to sink rapidly, perforated with small holes from the crocodiles' sharp teeth. Water quickly filled the armour, and Tom started to struggle with movement. Suddenly, Art spotted a cave at the water's edge, just tall enough for them to swim into. "There's a cave! We can seek shelter there, or maybe even find a way into the castle!"

Now swimming underwater, they found the cave's bottom littered with debris and junk. Apparently, this was some sort of sewage tunnel from the castle. Once inside the cave, they managed to surface. The cave expanded and was lit with torches, and a staircase on one side led out of the water. They tried to climb up as quietly as possible, but the armour, now completely filled with water, couldn't

get up on its own. The dragon slowly dragged him up and set him on the stairs. The armour leaked water, spraying it in all directions. While the armour was draining, the dragon ran up the stairs and found a passage leading into the mountain.
"Come on, we should go this way," he whispered. When Tom was emptied of all water, they both sneaked into the tunnel. It seemed to lead upward, hopefully towards the castle.
"This is the best way," said Art.

Tom thought that since there was no other way, it could also be the worst way, or the longest, or the finest. Tom realised that everything is relative.
"I wonder how Gecko is doing," pondered the dragon. "He would have been handy to have now, especially since you seem to have something thoughtful to say."

The cold air in the tunnel made steam billow from the dragon's breath. It was thanks to these vapours that they, at the last moment, noticed the narrow beams of light blocking their path.
"Stop! What's this?" wondered Art. "Look! There's something fishy here!" A faint light shone in slim beams across the tunnel passage. On the sides of the walls, they saw five small holes, aligned from floor to ceiling. Far inside the holes on one side, candles were burning, and on the opposite side, a hen sat in each hole, staring intently at the fire. Art pondered and examined the arrangement carefully, avoiding breaking any of the light beams.

"There are candles burning inside the holes... and on the corresponding side there are...", the dragon darted to the other side of the passage, "...a hen in each hole. A hen," he whispered. The dragon thought silently for a moment and then made a guess.
"This must be some kind of alarm system. If any of the hens no longer see the light on the other side, then they warn in some way, perhaps by clucking. There must be guards somewhere nearby. We can't get past." If they had taken one more step, they might have had five clucking hens in the tunnel, and who knows what that would have entailed.

Carefully contemplating their next move, Art and the dragon realised they needed to be exceptionally clever to bypass this unusual security system. The challenge was not just avoiding detection, but also not disturbing the hens, which required a delicate balance of stealth and ingenuity.

They sat down in the passage. They were so close to entering the castle, yet it was fortunate they hadn't triggered the alarm. Should they turn back now? Return to the crocodiles?
No, there had to be a way.
Art pondered and then had a small stroke of genius, or rather, a light bulb moment.
"I have my little flame," he thought. The dragon was always full of ideas. He lay down, lit the tip of his tongue,

and positioned the small flame right in front of the lowest hen. Art waved his hand behind it to demonstrate that his excellent idea worked. He put his hand in the way of the light, and nothing happened.
Now there was one less light beam in the passage, the lowest one was gone. He signalled to Tom to crawl, to pass under the remaining four light beams. Art tried to speak while keeping his tongue out.
"Crawl under now!" he urged the armour. Tom lay on his stomach and pulled himself under the light beams. There were no problems for him to pass.

Then it was the dragon's turn to get under, still with his tongue in place, which proved to be considerably more difficult. He twisted his body under the lowest light beam without changing the position of the flame on his tongue. It was very difficult to twist the body while keeping the head still. The dragon was also much thicker around the belly than Tom was. It was one of those moments when it was good that Tom couldn't speak. Otherwise, he would surely have, unknowingly, made a very inappropriate comment.
Art struggled with his large frame. Once his entire body had passed, he carefully retracted the flame and his tongue. The light from the other side of the tunnel could now shine on the hen again, which apparently hadn't noticed anything.
"That's it, easy as pie."

They continued through the tunnel, climbing many stairs. It was cold and damp in the narrow shaft, and torches on the wall were few and far between. Sometimes the passage widened into small rooms. One level was filled with rooms secured by bars, a dungeon. It was dark, but they could make out people lying on the floors in some of the cells. They could sense a quiet cough and some heavy breathing.

The bright light was blinding as they emerged into the courtyard. Not a soul was in sight; they were completely alone. There were towers, lots of towers, and many looked the same. It appeared entirely different from the courtyard than from the outside. They wandered around the courtyard, clueless about which tower they had heard the princess in.
"Which tower could the princess be in? I can't remember."
The dragon began to feel the doors and nodded at Tom.
"Try that door, is it locked too?" They felt all the doors, and all were locked. The dragon turned to Tom.
"You must go out again and check in which tower we heard the princess. We can't break open all the doors. We need to know which tower to enter."
The empty armour threw out its arms and shook its head; it had no idea, having hung terrified in the dragon's fangs when they were outside.
"Off you go now, off with you," the dragon urged. Tom started to walk but stopped after a few steps. How was he going to get past the hens? He turned around, looking at the dragon. How could he make the dragon understand

that he couldn't get past the hens? The armour bent forward, placed his arms behind his back, and flapped them gently while pecking around. His pantomime skills were something of a specialty; anyone could see he was imitating a chicken. They had seen many hens on the farms of the Perghoola plain. The dragon pretended to ponder and then smiled in amusement at the performance. When he tired of the entertainment, he said:
"I understand, you're thinking of the hens in the tunnel. You stay here, I'll go instead."

The dragon retraced their steps back the way they had come. Tom couldn't do much; he sat down in a corner and waited. He looked around; everything seemed calm except for a faint thumping sound.
The stamping of the guard patrol grew closer, and Tom began to feel uneasy. He couldn't literally twist around, but his worry increased. There was nowhere for him to go, and running would only arouse suspicion. He chose to sit still, hoping they wouldn't notice him.
A commanding officer and seven soldiers marched past, and none seemed to take notice of the armour. The leader walked slightly behind the troop, stretching himself repeatedly, as if he wanted his stature to rub off on the troop. It didn't seem to make any difference. After they had passed, he turned to Sir Notalot.
"Don't just sit there idling."
It was a captain, and captains have the authority to put all soldiers to work. "Into the ranks with you, we need more hands for patrol."

Tom nodded, got up, and joined the line, and the entire patrol began marching towards the gate. Since he couldn't say anything, he had no choice but to follow along. They went out through the gate, across the bridge. The armour quietly sighed as he realised that he would once again have to climb up the dreadful hill.

Meanwhile, the dragon had managed to sneak past the hens and emerged near the water. He found a small ledge at the mouth of the cave, but he couldn't see the tower from there. Looking up, he only saw steeply sloping walls and cliffs. His main concern now was how to cross the river.

In the river, some crocodiles were swimming, while others basked on the opposite shores. Jumping in here would be suicidal. He pondered and then suddenly came up with a fantastic idea. He positioned himself on all fours, gaping and trying to resemble a crocodile, albeit a rather plump one that had just had a Hearty meal. He stood like this for a while, licking his lips. The crocodiles in the river now swam by enviously.

Aha, thought the dragon, it seems to work; they think I am a crocodile. Maybe one that just ate whatever was sitting here on the cliff. Now, I just have to swim across like a crocodile. He plunged in and swam as he had seen the crocodiles swim, slithering and gliding. None of them paid him any attention.

Once on the other side, the dragon quickly climbed up onto the shore, crawling on all fours and passing the sunbathing crocodiles.

Art now started looking for the tower they had seen earlier, the one with the crying princess. He was still too low to see over the wall, so he continued crawling up the slope to get a better view. If only he could spot the tower, he would then be able to find some landmarks to locate the building within the castle.

Tom, meanwhile, struggled up the hill. It was exhausting, and the armour was not the only one who thought so. Most of the soldiers had traversed the hill many times. The little soldier next to Tom was of a significantly more alert classification. He often looked around, scanning the surroundings as soldiers should but seldom do, and suddenly he spotted something down by the water. Tom looked in the same direction and saw Art running around among the rocks below. The soldier turned to alert the commander, but before he could open his mouth, Tom lunged in front of the soldier, causing him to trip over the armour. This resulted in the whole troop collapsing into a big pile. A very small person quickly and unnoticed ran up and snuck behind Sit Notalot's visor.
"Hiya, mate," he whispered to the armour. "I was just wondering when you'd come to fetch me."

The dragon, hearing the commotion and clatter on the road above, quickly hid behind a rock. He had just spotted the tower where he had earlier heard the princess crying. Noting a helmet with large yellow and blue plumes in one of the tower windows, he was confident he would find it. "Now it's just a matter of getting back inside," Art thought, casting a glance up the road. He wondered what had happened up there. Best to sneak cautiously.

The soldier who had seen Art in the field below now pointed at Tom, still lying on the ground.
"He fell like a football player," he complained. "For no reason, he just lay right in front of me."
The commanding officer felt he was losing control of the situation, one of the worst things an officer can experience. He quickly tried to restore order.
"Line up!" he bellowed.
"But I saw something strange in the field down there."
The soldier pointed, and everyone moved to the edge, curiously looking down into the valley. Far below, they could see a crocodile crawling back into the water.
"A crocodile!" exclaimed Gecko.
The captain had had enough. "Enough of this. Line up!" he bellowed, muttering in disapproval about everyone going to the edge without his command. Being in charge was very important to our captain. The soldier who had tripped tried once more to make himself heard, insisting it wasn't a crocodile he had seen.
"But..." he began, only to be sharply cut off by the now highly irritated captain.
"Forward march! We have a long patrol ahead of us tonight!" he shouted angrily. "Anyone who utters another word will be thrown over the edge to the crocodile down there."

The steadfast soldier chose to remain silent. The patrol eventually got organised and continued their arduous march up the hill.

Art, in the water, heard the soldiers regroup and continue their march up the road. Swimming like a crocodile, he continued across the river into the water cave. Unbeknownst to him, Sir Notalot had now joined the patrol he had noticed on the heights.

Art was becoming quite adept at passing the hens, but this time something unexpected happened. Just at the critical moment, a claw got stuck between the stones on the floor. He couldn't get free. He couldn't move his head and tried to see what had caused him to get stuck. After much straining and poking, the claw finally came loose.
"Phew," he exhaled, inadvertently extinguishing the small flame on the tip of his tongue.
The effect was immediate; the hen began to cluck loudly and insistently. Terrified by his mistake, the dragon stood up, and the sound of five wildly clucking hens echoed through the castle's passageways.
Arfeudo, the officer on duty at the castle, had a relatively comfortable assignment, especially when almost all the soldiers were out on patrol. It was an opportunity for a little nap, which he had taken that afternoon.
Marshal Arfeudo was a small man with great authority, evident from his helmet adorned with large yellow and blue plumes. He also had more markings on his shoulders and chest indicating his high rank.

Hearing the hens, he had jumped up, approached the window, donned his ornate headgear, and, terrified, ran out onto the courtyard. He immediately headed to the bell tower and started ringing the bells. The sound echoed far and wide, signalling that the castle was under attack or that intruders were present. Now, all he had to do was wait for the soldiers to assemble in the courtyard, then he would dare to leave the tower.

The situation was rapidly escalating. The castle, now alert to a possible threat, was about to become a hive of activity. Art, realising the magnitude of his error, knew he needed to act quickly. The castle would soon be swarming with soldiers searching for the source of the disturbance. He needed to find a hiding spot or a way out of the immediate area before he was discovered. In the midst of the chaos, he also wondered about Tom's whereabouts and hoped he was safe.

As the bell continued to ring, Art scurried through the passageways, seeking a place to conceal himself or perhaps even find another route that could lead him closer to the princess or out of this increasingly perilous situation. Meanwhile, soldiers, roused by the alarm, would soon be converging on the castle from all directions. The race against time and discovery was on. Soldiers, having reached the edge of the forest when the alarm sounded, were immediately addressed by the captain. "Alarm

Back to the castle, we're under attack!" The soldiers instantly turned around and marched quickly down the road. Tom, yet again, had to run down the dreadful hill.

Art emerged onto an empty courtyard, rushing immediately to the spot where he had left Tom, but it was empty. "Where has Tom disappeared to?" Art couldn't understand where the armour had gone and began to search the yard.
The dragon didn't have long to search before he heard soldiers rushing over the bridge.Where should he go? He knew most doors were locked and the soldiers would likely run down the path he had just come up, towards the still clucking hens.
He found a barrel in the courtyard but couldn't squeeze into it and realised he couldn't hide behind it either.
In a corner stood a wooden cart, its slender spokes and thin slats around the load offering no cover, but he found straw on the flatbed. The dragon crawled into the straw and hurried to place strands of grass over the parts of his body that were still visible. Now, all he could do was hope that his camouflage would work.

The guard patrol rushed into the castle. At the same moment, not far from Art's hiding spot, a door opened. A small military figure, Marshal Arfeudo, with large blue and yellow plumes on his helmet, stepped out and walked determinedly towards the soldiers. Art whispered to himself, "There's the building we're looking for, but where is my old armour now?”

The dragon cautiously looked around. Soldiers were everywhere, and Art didn't expect Tom to be among them, so he didn't look for him. Not much to do, he thought, but wait until everything calmed down.

Every soldier was ordered to search for the intruder, with most being directed to the dungeon corridors. Tom, with Gecko inside, was assigned to search the courtyard. Eventually, they approached the cart where the dragon was hiding. Luckily, it was our friends who inspected the cart, for there was more dragon than straw on it.
"There you are," said Gecko from inside Sir Notalot. He was amazed at all his two friends had accomplished during the short time he had been away.
It's me," said the dragon, quickly brushing off the straw in the belief that otherwise they wouldn't recognise that it was him. He jumped down to the ground and looked joyfully at his friends. "And I know which tower we need to go up," he said proudly. "That one!" The dragon pointed to the tower where he had seen the man with the blue plumes. They rushed to the door and felt the handle, but of course, it was locked. How were they going to get in?
They circled the entire building, but there was no other way in. The dragon sat down with his back against the door and sighed.
"What do we do now? We can't exactly ask someone to open it. Besides, it seems everyone is looking for me."
Gecko poked his head through the visor, looked up at the tower, and exclaimed, "Wait! I hear something inside…"

They heard heavy footsteps, someone walking down the stairs. Suddenly, this someone stumbled and tumbled down the stairs.

The dragon winced with each thud as the person crashed down the stairs. One final loud thump, and the person hit the floor just behind the closed door.

A sword slid halfway out through the door, right under the dragon's nose. Before the dragon even had time to jump away, the sword started to wiggle back and forth, as the man inside was apparently eager to retrieve it. Art jumped aside, narrowly saving his nose. The sword disappeared back in, and Tom and the dragon sneaked away as they heard keys in the lock from the inside.

The door opened ajar, a bruised guard stepped out, took a few steps. He scanned the courtyard as if to check if anyone had seen his clumsy descent. The armour and the dragon then took the opportunity to sneak into the tower behind him. The first room was dark, and they hid under the curved stone staircase that began near the door. The clumsy soldier took out his keys again, slammed the door shut, and locked it.

With utmost caution, the dragon and the armour began to sneak up the spiral staircase. They passed several floors with small chambers. Beds stood neatly in a row.

"Nothing here! On to the next floor," urged Art.

In addition to the bedrooms, there were also rooms that looked like dining halls. No princess, no prison cells. They started to quicken their pace, and as they approached the eighth floor, Gecko poked his head out. "Stop the carousel, I'm getting sick."

They rushed on and soon reached the end of the staircase, finding themselves in a bell tower. The room had large openings on the sides, and in each opening hung a large bell. In the middle was a hole for the ropes used in bell ringing. Art ran around, frantically searching for the princess, even peering inside the bells. He was baffled. "But where is the princess?”
They all realised that they must be in the wrong tower. This was confirmed by the sobs they heard coming from the adjacent tower. Art quickly recognised the sound; he had heard it before. "There! She's in that tower!" he said, nodding towards the neighbouring tower. For some reason, they had entered the wrong tower. How it had happened, they didn't know.
"The door is locked down there," the dragon pointed out. "We'll have to find some way to get across."
Tom rushed down a staircase and quickly returned with a rope. Gecko was silent inside the visor.
"We can throw it over and climb." The dragon made a loop and tried to throw the rope over. He aimed for the stones in the row that ran along the top of the tower. Even though the building was slightly lower than the tower they were in, the rope only made it halfway before falling down. Art hauled the rope back up. He gave it his all in one last attempt, but it wasn't enough. The distance was too far. Art thought about how they had crossed the ravine. Art looked at Tom, who was thinking the same thing.
"No, not again," Gecko screamed from inside the armour. Art calmed him down and presented another idea.

"If we have a weight at one end, then we can swing the rope over." He looked around; the bells were far too heavy. Besides, it would be hard to use them without making noise. Art looked at the empty armour.
"You'll be perfect."
The armour just shook its head. He looked out over the edge, and then he started to shake all over, sounding like a cutlery drawer.
"I don't think he wants to," Gecko commented.
Despite the concerns, Art firmly tied the rope around the feet of the Shaking Knight, dropping Tom down the side of the building, with Gecko still inside the armour. With great care, Art lowered the armour down the outside of the tower. Manoeuvring a rope wasn't easy, especially with small, claw-like hands.
Halfway through the descent, a knot appeared in the rope, causing Art to lose focus and, subsequently, his grip. Tom plummeted headfirst. The rope whipped around on the roof, matching the frantic whirl of Art's arms trying to catch it. Just as the armour was about half a meter from the ground, the dragon managed to catch the end of the rope with his mouth, dangling over the edge. He carefully backed up onto the roof and grabbed the rope with both hands.
"There, perfect distance for swinging," he said and began to swing the rope. Tom swung back and forth, still shaking his head. With each swing, the armour moved closer to the other tower, then flew across to the other side at full speed.

"Help, I want off!" squeaked Gecko from inside the armour.
Art, undeterred, kept swinging. Perhaps he didn't hear Gecko's cries, or he didn't want to stop now that he had gained such good momentum.
Now, the armour was swinging very close to the other tower, and Sit Notalot stretched his arms out towards the ledge with stones. He managed to grab hold and hung on. Gecko immediately jumped onto his arms and hopped over to the roof of the building.
Metal gloves are not designed for grip, and Tom began to slide. Gecko grabbed him, trying to hold on, but it was no use. Tom lost his grip and flew back with full force, swinging over to the other side again.
Shortly after, he came flying back with even more speed and this time managed to get a firm grip on the stone edge. He was able to get one arm over and clumsily climbed onto the roof, eagerly encouraged by Gecko.
They had succeeded.
Tom turned around and saw Art giving a thumbs-up from the other side.

With trembling hands, Tom untied the knot around his legs and then tied the end of the rope to the stone blocks that bordered the roof of the tower. Art tightened the rope on his side, stretching and tying it securely. Then, the dragon carefully stepped out onto the rope. This should go well, it was both shorter and less high than when they crossed the ravine. If any of the guards had seen this, they probably wouldn't have believed their eyes. A large chameleon tightrope walking between two towers right over the castle courtyard.

Quietly cheered on by his companions, Art confidently continued stepping across the rope. When Art finally climbed over and they began to inspect the roof, they realised that the tower they were on had no staircase; it was just a roof. With a heavy tone of disappointment, Art noted, 'There's no staircase here, no way in or out!
They would have to climb down the outside to get away. As Art and Gecko pondered this problem, Tom silently moved towards the rope. Wanting to prove himself, he began to balance his way back across to the other side. His idea was to go back, undo the rope, and bring it back with him.
Tom had a fondness for ropes, and he had already made it halfway across when Art noticed his reckless endeavour. "What are you doing? Come back immediately," he whispered, not wanting to alert the guards, though he would have preferred to shout.
Despite Art and Gecko's quiet pleas, Tom continued his task. He had walked a tightrope once before, and it had gone well then. He thought retrieving the rope shouldn't be too difficult. He had wanted to do this at the ravine, but Art had stopped him then. Now, nothing could hinder him; this time, he would retrieve the rope.
As Tom reached the far side, he started to untangle the rope, his fingers working quickly. But in a sudden flash of realisation, he understood his grave error. It was too late – the moment the rope slackened, Tom found himself

succumbing to gravity, plummeting downwards unavoidably He grabbed the rope tightly in a reflex. The rope stretched taut, and the armour swung back with full force, crashing into the gate on the courtyard below. The wooden gates were sturdy and could withstand a lot, but an armour hurtling at full speed was too much; the gate shattered with a loud crash.

"No! You mad, foolish, metal buffoon!" Art yelled, unable to keep his voice down any longer. Watching the armour get smashed below, he realised how fond he had grown of him. His life had changed so completely since the armour had clomped into his treasure chamber. The sight of the damaged armour, a companion in their adventure, struck a chord in Art's Heart, underscoring the unexpected bond they had formed. Never before had Art felt or cared for another being in such a way; it was a wonderful feeling, yet so terrible when things went wrong. Raised to amass a formidable treasure, that had been the most important thing for a dragon. But now, Art had found something he valued more than all the treasures in the world. The concern he felt for Tom was much greater than any he had previously experienced when he left his treasure unguarded.

He just hoped that Tom was alright.

Completely immobilised, the armour lay amid the remnants of the shattered gate. One arm had come off but, apart from a few dents, he had survived the crash

relatively unscathed. Tom, dazed, couldn't get up on his feet to run away.
Eventually, Tom gathered himself and felt relatively okay. Given the many soldiers scattered throughout the castle searching for the intruder, it didn't take long for a group to gather around him. Weapons drawn, they were tense, curious, proud, and nervous, their knees shaking as they tried to look important. They believed they had finally found the intruder and each wanted to claim the credit for the capture. They all crowded around the eerie knight in armour.

The dragon and Gecko chose to stay out of sight when Sir Notalot was captured. The guards took charge of the armour, forcing him to stand up. Then they circled the captive to show him off to the commanding officers. The dragon tried to see where they were taking the prisoner, but all he could see was that they disappeared behind a large building. One of the soldiers didn't follow; instead, he ran into the building through the shattered gate.

The dragon, with Gecko on his shoulder, began to climb down the rope. They passed close to the window where they had previously heard the princess crying.

Finally.

The opening was a bit away, so they couldn't see inside. They heard the princess's sobs and heard a man enter the room.

"We have captured the intruder, an unknown knight in armour," said the guard proudly. "We have taken him to the dungeons."

"The dungeons," whispered Art. "Good, now we know where Tom is."

They didn't hear more but continued to climb down; now they knew where Tom was being held captive. That was all they needed to know. Now their friend was the most important thing to them; princesses in distress would have to wait.

If only they had stayed by the window a little longer, they would have heard a woman's voice respond.

"That's good, soldier. What do we know about him?" inquired the woman.

"It's likely the same man who tried to get past our hens."

"Could he possibly be from far away?" the woman continued. "Ask if he has seen or knows of any dragons. He shall be punished for his intrusion into our castle, but if he can help me find a dragon, he will be set free."

The woman's voice belonged to a dragon, a female dragon, a Dragon Queen. This was her castle, and the soldiers were there to defend it, but also to search for other dragons. She had been searching for many years but had never managed to find another dragon.

She often sat and cried, saddened by her loneliness. She was increasingly resigned to the likelihood that she might be the last dragon in the world. She was a very beautiful and kind dragon, and her subjects were obedient, protecting her with their lives, for she was a beloved and fair ruler.

The two intruders, unaware of this, were sneaking towards the building where they had seen the guards disappear with their friend.

Sir Notalot sat alone on the floor of the prison cell. It was a small cell, with old and musty straw on the cold stone floor. Through the bars, he could see there were more cells, but all were empty. This was not the same dungeon they had seen when they first arrived at the castle.
A guard approached the cell, and the door creaked as he opened it.
"What are you doing in our castle, you damned thief and snooper?" roared the guard.
Tom looked up at the guard. The guard was angry and resolute, poking Tom's leg with his spear, feeling superior. He suspiciously eyed the emblem on Tom's chest, not recognising it.
"Where are you from?"
The armour remained expressionless. Even if he could have answered, he wouldn't have; he didn't want to reveal his friends, so he chose to look away.
"We're looking for a dragon; you'll be freed if you can help us," said the guard, prodding with his spear. Now he aimed at Tom's helmet. The armour didn't flinch, even though he was surprised when the guard started talking about Art.
The guard backed out and slammed the door shut.

"Then you'll just have to stay here until you talk."
It might be a long time before I talk, Tom thought, and managed a cautious smile on his plate mask while the guard locked the door with one of many large keys on his key ring.

Art and Gecko now headed to the prison that the dragon and Tom had passed on their way in. They ran down into the building and among the prison cells. They looked into every cell, but none of the prisoners were wearing armour.
"Tom can't be here; there must be more dungeons in the castle," said Art. They hurried back to the courtyard. There were several gates where the guards could have taken the prisoner.
They were surprised by footsteps in one of the openings and jumped behind a barrel just as four soldiers came rushing out. The small platoon ran on, not noticing the dragon trying to hide behind a barrel.

When the courtyard was quiet again, Art and Gecko crept towards the gate where the guards had emerged. Inside the gate, there was only a staircase leading downward, its length indiscernible. If they encountered anyone on that staircase, there would be no turning back.
They cautiously descended, initially slowly, but with each step, they grew bolder and eventually moved at a brisk pace. They should now be level with the gate where the dragon and the armour had once sneaked in.
Art couldn't recognise the place. When the staircase ended, they found themselves in a large, elongated hall

with a high ceiling. In the middle, there was a shaft of light that seemed to lead up to the courtyard. There were corridors along the long sides. The light only extended far enough to see a few meters into the corridors. They had no idea where to start looking.

Chapter 10:

An Unusual Escape

Sir Notalot was left alone in his cell, pondering what to do next. He will never be able to speak, no matter how much they prod with swords at me. But maybe I can still get out, he thought, and lay on his back just inside the cell door. He manoeuvred his left foot out by wiggling it back and forth. Then he stuck it out through the bars and placed it outside the door, outside the cell. Carefully, he looked around but there were no guards nearby.
The right foot made the same journey. The legs were disassembled, the plates separated and sent out through the bars. Then he reassembled the legs and feet on the outside of the bars, calmly and carefully.

The hip plates were detached, and Tom pushed them through the bars and attached them to the legs.
Next up were the back and chest plates. They were divided, sent out through the bars, and then put together.
Now, he began to struggle with movement. He removed his left glove and laid it out through the bars.
As he laid out his entire left arm and attached it to the shoulder piece, the arm on the outside began to assist.
Now, he took off his helmet, split it, pushed it through the bars, and put it together on the other side. Almost all parts were now placed outside the door.

Left in the cell was only a lifeless right arm. Tom inserted his arm, retrieved the remaining parts, and put them in place. Everything might not have been as good as before, but he held together and could move.

He was free.

But where should he go?

He looked around. He seemed to remember that the guard had gone to the right, so he did the same. The passage then turned left, and he followed the stairs upwards. He reached a long, narrow corridor lit from the side by small light slots near the ceiling. At the far end was a large wooden door, and in the middle of the corridor stood a knight in armour. Tom stopped; first, he was a bit scared, but then he noticed that the armour was on a pedestal. No danger, it must be an empty suit of armour, he thought. He walked slowly down the corridor, stopping at the armour to look. The armour was very old, rusty, and dusty. It bore the same emblem on its chest as the flag they had seen in the morning when they had hidden in the bushes, a dragon against a red background.
Voices were now heard from the staircase he had just passed, and at the same time, the door at the other end of the corridor opened.
There was nowhere to hide, so he quickly stood against the wall and remained perfectly still, eye to eye with the

armour. He thought he saw the armour blink at him, but it must have been a play of light when the door opened.

From both directions, soldiers now rushed in. The two from the basement were shouting and bawling.
"He has escaped, protect the queen, he might try another assassination attempt," were the shouts heard. The soldiers who had opened the door immediately turned around. One could hear them shouting and spreading the message. The soldiers from the basement passed by both suits of armour. The last one glanced at Tom and paused.
"What is this? Has this armour been here before? It looks like..." Before he finished his sentence, he lifted his sword and with violent force struck the side of Tom.
The armour collapsed just like any empty suit of armour would have. Parts flew around the corridor, bouncing off walls and floors. The armour was as empty as it ever could be.
"My mistake. Off with you now, we must find the intruder," he shouted and then realised that this was probably the intruder's armour.
"He has tricked us and taken off his armour. Be alert!"
The corridor fell silent once more as the soldiers disappeared through the door. Tom tried again to assemble himself, but the pieces were too far apart. The glove vainly attempted to reach the forearm plate but lacked the strength, slowly losing its power. The visor was knocked away, lying far down the corridor. The helmet lay lifeless, and the glow in his eyes slowly started to fade. One could

hear the faint crunching of the pieces trying to move, but after a while, everything became quiet and still.

The dragon and Gecko had peered into all the passages and couldn't decide which one to try first. Two of the tunnels sloped gently downwards, while the others continued straight into the darkness. The dragon lit its small tongue-tip flame and poked its head into the openings.

"Brilliant!" said Gecko.

The flame flickered in one of the tunnels, and they decided to try that one. They entered total darkness. The dragon's flame was weak, illuminating just enough for it to see where it was placing its feet but not much more.

The air grew colder and damper. The dragon felt uneasy, as if something unpleasant had happened. Its flame in the mouth dimmed and almost went out, now not even able to see its feet.

Was it just the air around them that made it anxious? It felt that its metal companion needed him, and it began to run.

The passage became brighter and brighter, appearing as if they were running up towards the light but still downward.

Suddenly, they came to a stop. They had reached a wall, with light streaming in through a large hole. Art poked his head out and blinked in the bright light.

Upwards was the sky, on the sides only cliffs, and below there was only water. They had no choice but to turn around and rush back. Art ran as fast as he could. When

they were almost back, footsteps were heard in the hall from where they had started.
They crept the last part, and when they arrived, they could see soldiers walking past. They tried another tunnel, but it too ended in a dead end. Art's flame had now completely gone out and couldn't be reignited; he no longer had any fire, and he was deeply worried about what this could mean.
They heard steps in the hall behind them again. This time it was louder. Shouts and clamour, but they couldn't make out what was being said.
They quickly hurried back and managed to see some soldiers rushing out of an opening they hadn't tried yet. When the hall became quiet, they decided to go down that passage. The soldiers continued running and shouting about the intruder, which Art and Gecko didn't pay much attention to. Once everything had quieted down, they sneaked across the hall and into the passage they had seen the soldiers emerge from. The passage was lit by torches and seemed promising. Now they must surely be on the right track.

The armour, or rather, all of Sir Notalot's parts lay scattered and motionless in the corridor. Would his short life end here, shattered and in pieces?
He had had a good life, having made two fine friends. They had had a lot of fun together. There was nothing he had done in his short life that he wished undone, and nothing he hadn't done that he wished he had managed to

do – that's just as important. But now, it seemed, it was over.
Then a new sound was heard, a faint metallic creaking barely audible. Old plates that had rusted together over many years. Joints that hadn't moved for centuries slowly began to change position.
The old armour that had stood motionless in the corridor began to move. There was a clank as a rusty old metal shoe hit the floor near Tom's breastplate. It creaked and groaned as the old armour slowly approached the lifeless helmet, turned it over, and carefully set it right.
Slowly, it gathered the breastplates and arm joints. The gloves and legs were also put in place. Piece by piece, the armour was painstakingly assembled. Once the armour was fully complete, the ancient suit knelt down and placed its hands on Tom's breastplate. Gradually, the glow in Tom's lifeless eyes began to return, there was a twitch in the metallic fingers as they started to come to life again.
The old armour stood up and with heavy steps walked back to its stone pedestal. The armour creakingly turned around and then all was quiet again. This was an effort like no other, and the rusty old plates would probably never be able to move again.

Sir Notalot sat up and looked around. He could remember being severely beaten. He had faint memories of the armour by the wall helping him find himself. He sensed that the armour had struggled free from its place to pick up his pieces and then brought him back to consciousness.

Tom stood in front of the old armour but noticed nothing unusual. It seemed like a dream, but Tom became more and more convinced that the old armour had indeed helped him come back to life.
He remembered the bottle he had received from Gandhini. He had stored it attached to the inside of his breastplate. Tom wanted to do something to thank the old armour for saving his life. He took out the bottle and looked at the label. Speak, it read on the bottle.
Tom had pondered a lot about what the text meant. Now he might get an answer, he thought, and poured the entire contents over the old armour.
Muffled voices echoed from the basement. Even more soldiers were on their way up, and this time it sounded like there were many of them.
The tramping of boots resonated in the corridor, and Tom realised he couldn't stay here, although he was curious to see—or rather, hear—if the magical liquid had worked.

Tom ran towards the door at the end of the corridor, opened it, and found himself in a long, dark passage that gradually ascended. It was dark except for a torch that shone in the distance. He hoped the passage would somehow lead out since the guards had gone this way. He closed the door and continued on; at the torch, the passage turned to the right, and he paused.
He heard someone or something around the corner. He tried to be quiet, but an armour suit can be difficult to silence completely. But what does it matter, he thought, the soldiers will any minute burst through the door behind

me, and then it's back to the prison, this time accompanied by guards.

Indeed, a patrol was making its way up from the basement behind Tom. Two officers led the way, followed by ten soldiers. Arfur, the smaller of the two officers, insisted they continue searching in the basement. He wore a thick, dark leather jacket, with arms and legs clad in iron. Ratophus, the other officer in a large breastplate, believed they had orders to join the others in the courtyard. But Arfur was very adamant.

"I know he's still down here somewhere in the basement."

"It doesn't matter," Ratophus replied. "We're to meet with the others in the courtyard immediately."

"But there's no way he could have gotten past the guards," Arfur said, glancing down the passage as if expecting to see the intruder walking up behind them.

"He must be down here."

"You're right, let's turn back," he heard in response as they passed the old armour. Arfur was quick to halt the patrol and ordered a complete turnaround. But Ratophus was confused.

"What are you doing? Who said we should turn back?"

"You agreed we should go back," Arfur replied.

The soldiers had already turned and began heading down the stairs. Arfur followed suit.

"Stop," Ratophus said, placing his hand on Arfur's shoulder. "You can't decide that we are going back down."

Now he was starting to get angry, and above all, he was afraid that the soldiers would think he wasn't in command. The idea of this smaller man taking charge over his soldiers was unacceptable, even if he happened to be right.

Arfur didn't turn around. He believed that Ratophus had agreed to turn back. What a strange man to change his mind so suddenly.

"Halt!" Ratophus shouted, and then a voice was heard.

"This little man has no say here."

Arfur might be small, but he had strong fists. Ratophus was about to experience this firsthand, and quickly a fight broke out.

The old armour, of course, had spoken for the first time in its long life, choosing its words wisely. It successfully prevented Tom from being discovered on the other side of the door. Speaking took a lot of effort, and it would be a very long time before it spoke again.

The dragon and Gecko hurried into the passage that the soldiers had left so hastily. Now they both believed they were finally on the right track. They had thought so many times during the day, but feelings exist only in the moment, so at this instant, this felt absolutely right. Art also thought of Tom, resolving not to give up now; they had to find Tom quickly. Art was convinced that Tom was in grave danger.

Soon, they both heard footsteps in the corridor ahead of them, steps that abruptly stopped. The passage made a sharp turn at the torch, and they both continued stealthily, backs pressed tightly against the wall.

Left foot forward, quiet, no sound. Next foot, quiet, wait, there was that strange sound again.
Art and Gecko couldn't understand what they were hearing. Art was now at the corner. He decided to take a look. He thrust his head out to get a glimpse and was startled to see a man in armour sneaking from the other direction. He quickly pulled his head back, pressing himself against the wall.
Gecko wondered what he had seen, for it took a moment before Art realised who the man in the armour was.
The armour, of course, was Sir Tom Notalot.

The joy was immense now that they had found each other again. Gecko immediately leapt over to Tom to recount what had happened.
"I'm so happy to see you," laughed Art. "We thought you were dead in the dungeons."
"He's been very close to death indeed," Gecko replied. "I'll tell you more soon, but we mustn't forget that we have a princess to rescue."
Art started thinking about their original mission again. "It's going to be tough now, with all the guards looking for a criminal who blows doors open with just his body."
He now understood the soldiers' shouting. "The escapee they're searching for, that's you?"
Tom nodded uncertainly, not quite understanding whether what he had done was good or bad.
"It doesn't matter," said Gecko. "Come on, we need to save the princess. But first, we need to get out of here."

They heard a commotion on the other side of the door behind Tom. It sounded like a fight, and they decided to quickly head in the opposite direction.

Chapter 11:
Many Small Friends

Gecko recounted Tom's adventure after he had smashed the gate, about the guards who took him away. About being promised freedom if he revealed the dragon and how he then escaped from the prison. Tom of course thought that the guard was asking about Art when he was questioned about knowing any dragon.

The courtyard was a hectic place right now, swarming with soldiers running in all directions. It seemed impossible to cross unnoticed to the princess's tower. Moreover, two guards stood in front of the smashed gate. They decided to try and find a passage under the courtyard instead.

They went back into the building, as they would be quickly spotted in the courtyard. Inside the building, they found a passage they had never been in before, and it seemed to lead towards the tower.
They had no trouble stepping over the small barrier that stood in the middle of the opening. It was dark, so the dragon lit its small flame. Now it shone brightly and convincingly. The warm light filled the dark tunnel. It was almost eerily quiet; they could barely hear the commotion ongoing in the courtyard. They entered, initially

cautiously, then quickened their pace as they ventured deeper into the tunnel.
Too late, they realised that the floor suddenly ended, and both tumbled over the edge. Art was so startled that his flame went out. They rolled around in the darkness, sometimes hitting the sides as they fell, faster and faster.

After what felt like an eternity, they all landed in a large pool. They plunged deep into the pitch-black, cold water. They quickly surfaced.
Gecko hurried to slip out through the visor and sat on the helmet of the armour. He was wet and terrified.
Art lit his flame, and they could now see a hole straight up from where they had fallen.
They were in a water-filled cave. They couldn't see where it ended to the sides. None were injured after the violent fall, but they had no idea of the direction anymore, except upwards and downwards, of course.
Art grabbed Tom and swam away, eagerly cheered on by Gecko. They soon reached the end of the cave. Unfortunately, it was just a bare wall; there was nothing to climb onto. Art decided to swim to the left. They slowly followed the wall. Sometimes the ceiling was low, sometimes the wall disappeared. They swam in a bit but only to discover that it was a dead end too. They swam on; there had to be a way out.
They passed several openings, but all turned out to be dead ends. Eventually, Gecko pointed out what they all had suspected, that they were swimming in a circle.

"We've passed this place before," he said, pointing at the low ceiling and the bulge they had passed an hour ago. They were trapped; there was no way out. Tom, still perforated by crocodile teeth, sank deeper and deeper. Gecko had jumped off the helmet and was now crawling on the cave wall. There, he felt much safer than on a sinking suit of armour in deep water.

Art saw two small bright dots in the ceiling a bit away. They flickered off and on. He nodded to the others to check if they saw the same thing. They looked like eyes in the darkness, and when he looked up again, they had come a bit closer.
"Wait here," said Gecko. "I'll be right back."
He climbed up the ceiling and continued towards the red lights. He crawled like a lizard on the wall, a talent none of the others had seen before. Art looked at Tom in surprise.
"What has he found now? This is not a nice place to wait."

They didn't have to wait long. Now there were four bright dots. It was Gecko coming back, still climbing on the ceiling. He was accompanied by another arm-length creature.
"This is Jamarar. He heard the splash and came to check if any crocodile had wandered into the cave system. He and several families of Limberiks live in a cave nearby."
"How did he get in if we can't get out?" the dragon immediately wondered. "Hello, by the way."

"Nice to meet you," said Jamarar. "You'll have to dive a little bit, then you'll come to our cave." He spoke quickly, just like Gecko. "Come, follow me."

They all followed Jamarar. Gecko in the ceiling, Art and Tom in the water. Suddenly, the little creature stopped. There were no walls or other landmarks around, just black water. "We have to dive here," Jamarar explained. "When you go down a bit in the water, you will see light at the end of the underwater passage." He pointed in the direction they should look. "Take a deep breath and follow me!" he said and disappeared into the water.

Art, Tom, and Gecko all dived into the cold water. They could see the light far away in the water-filled tunnel. Jamarar appeared as a dark silhouette, already a bit into the tunnel.
They all swam after him.

It quickly became brighter, and now they could see the surface of the water shimmering above them. They all swam upwards while releasing their breath. When they reached the surface, they took in fresh air. The armour had trouble reaching the surface; it had become completely waterlogged. They all had to dive down again and pull him to the surface.

They found themselves in a lit cave. The light came from a low opening on one side. Along the sides, there were ledges at water level. Higher up, there were shelves and

outcroppings of rock. Everywhere, miniature people sat, staring wide-eyed at them.
"Welcome to my home," Jamarar said proudly.

A bit above the water, there was a large ledge, and they all swam towards it. Tom struggled to stay afloat, and they all had to help get him up. All the Limberiks stared in shock as Art removed Tom's head to let the water drain out more quickly.

Once Tom was emptied of water, Art put his head back on, and Tom sat up and looked around.
Jamarar introduced his family: his wife Istra and their children Ival, Estol, Komsi, and little Alvan. The latter was no bigger than a palm, Art thought.

It was true that several families of the arm-length folk lived in the cave. It was rare for them to meet others from the outside, so now they were going to throw a feast.
First, they brought towels so Art and Gecko could dry off.
Gecko, Art, and Tom were treated as honoured guests in the Limberiks cave. The children eagerly came forward to dry Tom both inside and outside. Each ledge had sleeping spaces and small tables and chairs. There were no walls, and it seemed that walls were unnecessary because there was never any wind inside the cave. Art noticed a peculiar pile of rocks on each ledge. The neatly stacked stones didn't seem to serve any function at all. He wondered if it was an art piece. If so, then every Limberiks home was adorned with a similar sculpture.

The tables brought out for the feast were too small for the guests, but the problem was solved by having Art and Tom sit on the edge with their legs hanging over the water.

Everyone found it exciting to have a dragon and a suit of armour as guests, but Gecko was even more fascinating. Arm-length folk rarely visited each other. They were not a traveling tribe, but Gecko was an exception, and he immediately started recounting all the adventures he had been on.

After the meal was served, an array of delicacies filled the table, including mussels, small fish, large fish, crocodile eggs, and a seaweed salad. Both wine and water were poured generously, adding to the high spirits that seemed to rise up to the very ceiling of the cave. Gecko continued his stories, talking about his new friends and their so-called mission. Everyone was so captivated by his stories that no one noticed the crocodile that silently slipped into the cave. Perhaps it was attracted by the commotion of the feast, or maybe it was the smell of all the delicious food. A crocodile is hard to spot, swimming with only its eyes above the surface, sometimes completely underwater. This was a large crocodile, capable of swallowing a whole Limberik in a single bite.
Art saw it first and didn't know what to do; the ledge they were sitting on was not safe at all. A crocodile could easily climb up there. He stood up and was about to shout

when a little whistle was heard. All the Limberiks rushed to the nearest pile of stones and grabbed a stone in hand. Then they very accurately threw their stones right at the crocodile's head, or more precisely, right at its eyes. The crocodile struck with its tail and immediately turned around. The waves nearly reached the ledge where they sat. The waves propagated through the cave, splashing in different directions before finally calming down completely, and the water surface lay still like a mirror. Jamarar then explained that crocodiles have very short memories."
"They often swim in here just to be reminded that they're not allowed," he said, laughing.

No more crocodiles needed reminding that evening.
It slowly started to get dark, and torches were lit on the walls. The light from them reflected in the water, making it look like the walls were moving. Neither Tom nor Art had ever experienced anything as fantastic as this. A party with friends was new to them. The party never seemed to end, and many great stories were told that night.

In the morning, they were awakened by Gecko. Perhaps too abruptly, for Tom immediately hit his head on the cave ceiling. They had all slept very well, feeling safer than they had in a long time. Gecko spoke quickly, much faster than usual; he apparently had something important to say. Art calmed him down and asked him to start from the beginning. Gecko then excitedly explained that Jamarar had found something very good in the castle.

"He knows which tower we can find the crying female in, and he will help us get there."
"But first, breakfast," he yelled, echoing through the cave.

Satiated and content, they thanked all the families for the food and lodging, then followed Jamarar deeper into the cave. There was a hatch, and Jamarar waited to open it until everyone had arrived. When he slid the hatch aside, a tunnel appeared. Jamarar and Gecko immediately jumped through. Art had trouble with the size of the opening and got stuck. Jamarar and Gecko grabbed his arms and pulled from their side. Tom pushed as hard as he could from his end.
"Breathe out!" said Gecko. "Think thin."
Art's upper body and wings had made it through. It was his hindquarters that were too large, or as Art thought, the opening was too small for his backside.
"If we wait a day or two, it might be easier," said Jamarar. Gecko agreed without hesitation.
Art disliked that option. He struggled and shifted his entire belly forward so there wouldn't be as much left behind. He looked like a large, croaking frog. Once his belly had passed, it was relatively easy to squeeze his backside and legs through. Tom quickly followed.

They followed Jamarar through tunnels and passageways, sometimes through narrow corridors, often upwards, sometimes downwards. Jamarar knew his way around, which was fortunate, as he occasionally warned them about certain areas they shouldn't step on. Probably a bit

of thin flooring, Art thought, and stepped carefully past. They all thought Jamarar had taken a wrong turn when they reached a dead end, but Jamarar seemed calm.
"Take this and follow me," he said, pointing to a ladder against the wall. Art took the ladder under his arm. They turned back and walked a little way back. Suddenly, Jamarar stopped.
"Here we go up!" he pointed. Above them, they saw only stone.
"Art, put the ladder here and climb up," Jamarar instructed firmly.
Art did as he was told and climbed up.
"Now push upwards," continued Jamarar. Art pushed upwards, and a hatch loosened, letting him push further up. Light streamed down into the passage, clearly illuminating dust and mist swirling around in the draft from the opening.
"Keep going," Jamarar said. "Now gently slide the hatch aside."
Jamarar climbed up, over Art, to quickly slip through the hole in the cave ceiling. After a short while, he returned and whispered,
"Come up everyone, but be quiet. There are guards up here."

They entered what appeared to be a cellar with some boxes along one side. In an opening on the wall, a spiral staircase began winding upwards.
"Now I leave you," said Jamarar. "Close the hatch after me."

They thanked Jamarar, who quickly disappeared into the darkness. Art pushed the hatch back into place.
Art nodded to the others that they should start sneaking up the stairs.

Chapter 12:

The Dragon Queen

After only one turn in the staircase, they arrived in a beautifully decorated circular hall, quite different from the barracks they had explored the previous day. The whitewashed walls were adorned with paintings, and small windows were evenly spaced around the room.
The room once had a door, but it now lay shattered and scattered across the floor. Outside, two guards stood, probably replacing the broken door.
The dragon smiled at Tom as he cautiously made his way through the splinters on the floor.
"You've obviously been here before."
Gecko rushed toward the staircase leading further up the tower. However, they had not gone far when one of the guards turned around, saw Sir Notalot, and shouted, "Stop. Halt. It's him!"
"Go up and save the princess, I'll handle the guards," yelled Art, throwing himself out of the opening. Gecko stayed behind, not wanting to miss a good fight.
Reluctantly, Tom obeyed and ran up. After eight turns in the staircase, he entered a large hall. These walls too were white, with colourful draperies hanging on the sides and around the windows. Some plants were tastefully placed

on pedestals on one side, the other part of the room was elevated.

There, beside a window, among large pillows, sat a dragon, a dragon queen. She was gold-coloured, slightly lighter on the belly with a reddish hue along the sharp spikes on her back, her tail almost red. One could say that Tom was struck dumb with astonishment.

"Oh, here you are, knight," the dragon calmly stated. "Are you here to kill me?"

She didn't seem afraid, rather a bit relieved to finally see the intruder who had caused such a commotion in recent days.

"What are you after?" she continued. "I see you have no weapons. Or perhaps you plan to crush me with your bare hands?" the dragon said, shaping her hands like a ball. "Maybe in the same way you crushed the door?"

She began to find it strange that the knight said nothing. He didn't seem to be attacking, he didn't seem to be doing anything at all. The queen decided to be a bit more pleasant. Maybe that would work better.

"My name is Philomenia, what's yours?" she added, leaning forward to appear more personable.

Sir Notalot, of course, could not say anything. He tried to gesture, waving his hands towards the stairs, hoping that the dragon or Gecko would show up and explain. Tom had been successful with his mute acting in front of Art, but this dragon didn't seem to understand anything.

"I see you're waving your hands, are you a magician too?" wondered the queen, hoping the knight would start talking soon.
"Make me disappear, or turn me into a frog. I'm the last dragon on earth and I've suffered such loneliness you can never understand," she almost started to cry again. "As a frog, at least I wouldn't be alone. Go ahead now," Philomenia pleaded.
"But wait!" she suddenly exclaimed. "If you're a wizard, you could conjure up another dragon for me, a fine and beautiful dragon."
She had spent nearly her whole life searching for other dragons, trying many methods to find or even create one. She had fed porridge to frogs, given celery to small lizards, and let crocodiles swim in cognac, but none of these methods worked. She was willing to try any possible or impossible method, and letting a not-so-talkative wizard conjure up a dragon was a new and entirely untried approach.
"I shall reward you handsomely, you can take as much gold as you can carry from my treasure chamber," she promised. Yet, deep down, she knew it wasn't possible to conjure a dragon; it was all just a wishful dream. The Dragon Queen began to cry again, trying to hide her face in her hands.

Then, Art burst into the room. He had knocked down the guards and hoped that Tom had freed the princess.
The queen looked up and saw a dragon, exactly what she wished for, and not just any dragon, but the most

handsome dragon she had ever seen. Of course, she hadn't seen any others before, so that wasn't saying much. She saw not only another dragon but also fell in love.
"You did it! You did it!" she exclaimed, referring to the magical trick she had just witnessed.
"Sure, easy as pie," said Art, thinking of the guards he had just knocked down.
The misunderstanding didn't bother the two dragons. They were preoccupied with other things. Art was very taken with the female dragon; she was so beautiful, and so large. He had found himself a new treasure, a truly fantastic pearl. He walked up to the queen, bowed deeply, and kissed her hand.
"Artemisia Dracunculus, at your service."
"Philomenia," the queen stammered.

This was incredibly surreal for her. She had searched for years, never hearing or seeing anything that could lead to a dragon. And now, she had a living, breathing one right in front of her. She bit her tail to assure herself it wasn't a dream.
"Ouch."

This turned into a grand day at the castle, as the Dragon Queen had finally found her long-sought dragon, and of course, they were to marry. The celebrations for the upcoming wedding lasted five days. Art and Philomenia sat in the window, talking about life, the universe, and everything.

"It feels so good now," said Art. "Imagine, I've been sitting in my old cave for so many years, just collecting gold and treasures."
"Imagine it was you whom my soldiers were looking for," Philomenia said, laughing. "My soldiers could never search beyond Dragonspine Ravine. But they might not have found you anyway, hidden away in your old cave," she continued. They looked at each other, in the way that only love-struck dragons can.

Art thought back to the time in the cave and how Sir Notalot had appeared one day and changed everything.
"Where is Tom, by the way?" wondered Art, realising he hadn't seen the armour all morning. Tom was still his best friend, and they were usually together. Queen Philomenia, of course, was aware of the situation and replied,
"He's in the treasure chamber, picking as much gold as he can carry. That's what I promised him."
Art felt the need to set things straight.
"You know Sir Notalot isn't a magician, right?" he said somewhat sheepishly.
Philomenia laughed.
"Yes, I've come to realise that now, but I still stand by my word. We'll soon see how much he manages to take with him."

After a while, Tom slowly entered the hall. He walked leisurely, with heavy steps, carrying a very small chest. The queen looked up in surprise and laughed.
"Is that all you managed to carry?"

Then Tom set the chest down on the floor. He grabbed one of his legs and detached it. Gold and gems poured out, forming a large heap on the floor. When the gold reached the height of the armour's waist, it stopped flowing. Then, Tom took the leg he was holding and turned it upside down over his head. Diamonds cascaded over his head, looking like rain. Gecko jumped up and took a precious shower on the armour's head.
The queen looked on in amazement, then turned to Art, who was just smiling. He liked his friend and found this whole scene very entertaining. The queen then looked up at Tom, standing in a pile of her former fortune. She began to laugh, and everyone joined in her laughter. She had been cheated out of more than she had anticipated. But it didn't matter much to her; she had found something she valued far more, the handsome and kind dragon Art.

***

The forest was dark, as black as coal. The tall trees appeared as black silhouettes against the stars in the sky. In the distance, the sounds of the forest being torn apart could be heard. Trunks split, trees fell and were crushed. The sleeping birds woke up and fled screaming into the night sky. The ground vibrated and shook. Something very very large was moving through the forest.
It was as if the entire earth trembled as the mountain forced its way through the woods, the mountain where the dragon had his cave, Mount Dragon. The ground felt fluid and swayed like the swell of the ocean.

The trees fell like dominoes, everything crushed under its path. Its eyes were dark, cruel, filled with hatred. Worms emerged from the earth and tried to crawl away. Small rodents, snakes, frogs, and deer, all ran wildly to escape the colossus. Each step it took made the ground quake, thump, thump, THUMP!

Chapter 13:

A momentous visit

"Wake up, wake up immediately!" Art slept restlessly and was woken by a guard banging on the door.

He opened his eyes. It was early in the morning. Next to him lay Philomenia, sleeping calmly. The armour slept on the floor below, next to its pile of gold. The guard who entered was out of breath and looked very frightened.

"You won't believe me, but there's a mountain up on the hill. An angry mountain!"

The fear was evident on the guard's face. He looked as if something could come through the wall behind him at any moment.

"A talking mountain! It's asking for a dragon and a knight in armour."

The guard was absolutely right, there was an enormous mountain up on the edge, the colossus rumbled and roared. It swayed slowly and the bare trees on its sides dangled and swung. The mountain remembered the first thing it saw, it was the dragon and the knight, everything must be their fault. That's why it had now sought them out.

"Where is the dragon? Quarries and volcanic ash, I'll kill him!" it thundered. "And that little knight with the loose head, I'll mangle him!"

The mountain hated the dragon and the armour for awakening her, for she wanted to be a mountain, not a monstrosity.
"They turned me into this kind of clay, I want to be a mountain, hard and solid!" She leaned to one side, creating an opening under her, then closed the gap with such force that the ground bowed. "Granite and brick, I'll crush them when I catch them!"

The guards stood with spears drawn around the mountain but could do nothing. One cannot ward off a mountain with a spear, which really anyone can understand, but the soldiers had learned to act this way against intruders. The soldiers were afraid and reflexively did as they had learned, and that is the whole idea with soldiers, so it is not so strange.

When the mountain roared, trees and soldiers flew in all directions. Art and Tom walked up the hill. Art recognised his mountain, both from reality and from his nightmares. There were not as many trees on the mountain as he remembered, but it was the mountain where he had his treasure chamber. Many of the trees had yellowed, some had almost lost all their leaves. Some trees had broken off at the ground and roots lay visible around the sides of the mountain, it almost looked like hair.
"What do you want from us?" roared Art as they approached the mountain. He looked towards something that looked like two dark eyes on the mountain's slope. The mountain fell silent and became completely still.

Then she slowly leaned forward, becoming like a cliff above them.
Art and Tom took a few steps back.
"ARGHHHH. There you are, you slimy stalactites!" the mountain roared with all its might. The two negotiators were thrown backwards. The mountain twisted so that one of its eyes came very close to the dragon and the armour. The dark eye was full of life, an intense conscious gaze, like the eye of a whale.
"Roots and moraine, I'll kill you for what you've done to me!" the mountain continued furiously.
"You've made me a monstrosity. You transformed me into this. A thinking large stone, I have neither arms nor legs."
The mountain stretched up as if to gather new strength.
"Weathered mountain crevices, I want to be a mountain, not a boulder. What did you do to me? Are you wizards?"
"We haven't done anything! It must be a misunderstanding!" Art suggested, looking at Tom who seemed to understand nothing at all.
"Heart, my name is Heart!" she said, stretching herself up.
"I am a big lump with a lot of life, I feel that I have a pulse. I am Heart. You shall make Heart a mountain again," she roared. "Argh, the first thing I saw was you two. My entire insides collapsed and you ran out," the mountain roared, nodding at Sir Notalot. "This armour is not normal either, right?"
She scrutinised the armour, her eyes slowly moving up and down along it. As if she would find some defect or something else that could prove her claim."

"He's not made of flesh and blood either?" she continued. "Just like me?"
The mountain sent out an offshoot and lifted Art and Tom. The mountain's deeply set eyes looked darkly at them. Art tried to explain, to tell what he knew.
"It was some kind of magical liquid, but it wasn't us."
"WHO WAS IT THEN?" Heart roared so loudly that Art and Tom were again thrown backward and nearly fell off the cliff they were standing on.
"Say it then, cobblestones and landslides, who?"
"It was a knight," Art tried. "He tricked me into destroying my cave." Art tried to explain his innocence, but he had never talked down a mountain before."Why would I want to destroy my entire treasure chamber?" He stretched out his arms in a gesture of resignation and continued his defence. "The mysterious knight who fled with the princess probably knows what was in the bottles."
Heart pondered what Art had said, it sounded plausible, and she roared.
"Find him then!"

Chapter 14:
Council Meeting

The queen, Art, Gecko, and Tom were holding a council meeting in the hall. Where could they find the mysterious knight? Gecko was sitting on the table, playing with a pile of gold coins.

"But what about the princess? Maybe she knows who this knight is?" Gecko stood in front of Art and placed his arms on his hips.

"Where did you find the princess?"

Art looked sad and turned away, pondering. After a moment of hesitation, the dragon began to tell his story.

"She comes from a castle by the sea, in Dinghli, a land far to the east. I kidnapped her when she was alone in the forest." Art tried to recall his thoughts at that time. He continued, "She looked valuable, and she was valuable. It was a foolish thing to do, and I deeply regret it." The dragon looked up and saw his friends staring back at him in amazement. They found it hard to believe that the dragon they knew could do something like that. Art was ashamed.

"I don't want to show myself there again."

Gecko, unfazed by this, quickly added, "Those who live in the castle surely know who rescued the princess from your cave."
Gecko looked at Tom for agreement. The armour hesitated; he felt uncomfortable thinking about the knight who had "awoken" him and also tricked him into being a mere decoy. The dragon was not at all in agreement. He did not want to return to that castle under any circumstances.
"We'll never find him anyway," he added.

The queen didn't think their discussion was leading anywhere. Such old worries should be dealt with elsewhere. What has been has been; there's no point in brooding over it, but it can of course help in making better decisions for the future. Philomenia was used to making quick, and mostly wise, decisions.
"Listen to Gecko. I think the knight and the princess are together. If you find the princess, you'll find the knight, or maybe even a prince. The people in the castle surely know where the princess is, they might even live in that castle by the sea. Why don't you go there and find out?"

The spirit of adventure was not hard to arouse in the currently gloomy trio. Art relented when adventure was mentioned. He also thought Philomenia was right, everything she said seemed so wise.
"Okay, we'll leave tomorrow!" said Art, but quickly added, "But I won't talk to them or show myself when we arrive."

"I'm going too!" roared Heart when she heard about the expedition. Art tried to calm her and make her understand the absurdity of a mountain going on walks. Adventures can happen on mountains, but not mountains on adventures. "But it's a very long way to walk. You will slow us down. Wait here, we'll be back in a few weeks. Then we'll know how to turn you back into a normal mountain again." The mountain did not want to miss out at all. She was full of energy and saw no problems in walking to the distant sea in the east. "I can move day and night. Slate and moraine, I'm coming!"

The dragon began to realise that it was impossible to persuade a mountain, and this particular mountain seemed quite certain of her cause. "But you won't get across the ravine, and we can't take the detour up north, it would take half a year," the dragon said in another attempt to stop the large landmass.
"There is a crossing," the mountain replied briefly.
"There is not at all," objected the dragon. "We crossed it with ropes." Heart stamped, and the whole ground shook. "There is a crossing!" said the mountain, and with that, the discussion ended. "Of course, I'm coming, by all drilled wells, you won't fool me again!"
Art realised that it was not possible to persuade the mountain. It looked like a long walk with a mountain on their heels for the next few weeks, or even months "Okay, but we will keep our pace, we won't slow down just

because you're with us." "That's fine," said the mountain, and immediately seemed calmer.

In the following days, the dragon and Gecko spent their time in the castle's library looking for maps and other documents that could help them on their upcoming journey. Having previously traveled around the country mostly at random, they were now able to make a planned expedition. They found Dragonspine Ravine on the map, and the Trip River was also drawn. Unfortunately, it turned out that there was not much written about the land east of this area. Since the bridge had been destroyed, no one had crossed the ravine, and very few had managed to get past North Gap, the difficult passage in the north. They only found roughly drawn maps with a large sea in the far east. But the dragon had been there before, so they would probably find their way. He remembered that the castle was called Dawnfall and was beautifully located near the sea.

It was a fine spring day when they set off on their new adventure. Everyone was excited about the expedition, even Heart seemed satisfied; she did not complain, and the others interpreted this as everything being okay.

This was a planned journey with a clear goal. Besides the mountain, they were wonderfully good friends and knew they could trek together. They had packed a long rope because they were unsure if the rope over Dragonspine Ravine would still be in place. Art thought a lot about how the mountain managed to cross the ravine and what she meant by there being a crossing. After all, she had actually crossed the ravine, so something must have happened at the ravine.

Walking through the forest this time was no problem. The mountain's passage had left a wide firebreak through the entire country. Trees, bushes, and stones, everything was compressed into a smooth, fine path. They marched on at a good pace, with the mountain quickly catching up. Art, who had thought it inappropriate for Heart to come along, was the most eager and walked ahead. Perhaps he wanted to prove he was right, that Heart could not keep up with their pace.

In the afternoon, their progress slowed down; it became steeper as they climbed higher up the mountainside. They all longed to reach the crest so they could look out over the country on the other side. But with each hill they crested, there turned out to be another height a bit further on. The terrain began to get more uneven and rocky despite the mountain's levelling.

In the evening, they once again reached the top that they thought was the last hill, and this time it truly was. With the sun at their backs, they could now gaze out over the eastern lands. Far below, they could see Dragonspine Ravine. The mountain they had seen the last time they stood on this height was, of course, no longer there. Despite the great distance, they could see that Heart had

passed straight over the ravine. Her tracks were like scars in the landscape, clearly showing that she had reached the ravine, walked back and forth over it, and then continued on this side of the ravine.
"We shouldn't have left the rope behind," Tom thought.
Gecko laughed to himself as he imagined a mountain walking on a tightrope.

They walked downhill and didn't stop until they reached the forest. They cooked food and prepared the camp for the night. After eating, it was time to sleep. Despite having walked all day, they all found it difficult to settle down. Everyone was eager to see what had happened at the ravine. How was it possible that the mountain had crossed it?
In the distance, they could hear the heavy steps of a mountain on the move. This made it even harder to fall asleep. Now, they all lay waiting for Heart to reach them.

But what if she couldn't see them in the dark? They all listened for several hours until the mountain was really close. Heart slowed down, stopped, and everything became quiet. Somehow, she knew they were there in the darkness. But no one had the energy to ponder over it. It had become quiet, they were all tired, and they fell asleep quickly.

In the morning, everyone was eager to get moving. Heart had gone ahead of them and was already halfway to the ravine. She wanted to watch as they arrived and saw her crossing. She was proud of her creation.

It was evening when they reached Dragonspine Ravine. Indeed, there was a new crossing that hadn't been there the last time they were here. It looked as if the landmasses were being pushed downward and outward, eventually meeting to form a broad path over the chasm. Heart stood at the edge, pretending to look away, very proud of her construction.
"It took a few days," she said as they slowly stepped out onto what resembled a bridge. "But then the land began to yield and was pushed out by my weight."

They walked tensely across the isthmus. Far below them, the water flowed just as before. When everyone had crossed, it was Heart's turn. She stepped out onto the isthmus, and the ground cracked. She walked calmly on. Gravel and stones tumbled down the sides towards the water far below. The bridge sank a few more meters during her crossing. When she finally made it across, the structure seemed even more stable.

Heart never crossed the bridge again after this, and the connection remained for many hundreds of years. It became an important trade route between the two countries. The bridge later came to be known as Heart's Bridge in common parlance. Many people believed it was named so because it was situated right in the middle of the two countries. However, others held a firm opinion that the bridge symbolised the love shared between two individuals.

Chapter 15:
The City of Hagriven

Gecko and Art, having studied maps, now wanted to take a southerly route, near Hagriven, the great city in the south and the country's capital. It would be a shorter walk to take the route via Wyrmville, they pointed out. Additionally, Art was reluctant to pass through Wyrmville, but for a different reason.

They often traveled on roads, finding it much more comfortable than navigating through rough terrain or winding paths. Whenever they encountered people, Art would hide at the side of the road. Heart moved more to the north, on the plains. They all agreed it was unwise for her to cut through forests and create clearings, as it would only attract unwanted attention. People could easily become frightened by a wandering mountain, which is entirely understandable. At the same time, Gecko pointed out, she could become hard to detect if she stopped and stood still. People moving in unfamiliar territories didn't react to a mountain, but those walking in their home areas would certainly find it unnerving to see a mountain where there used to be farmland.

After several days of walking, they approached Hagriven. This was the largest city in the land, home to the king and his armies. The city was built on a low hill, and its white walls ran around the entire hillock. Inside, there were many small houses at various elevations, and on the plains around the city were some larger farms.

From a distance, they could see the western gate, a blue gate, one of the four entrances to the city.

As they stood admiring the city, they heard a cart approaching from behind. Art hurried off the road and curled up. Tom stayed put, and Gecko hid inside the armour. Usually, people just passed by, and Tom would shake his head if offered a ride.

"Hey buddy," was heard as the wagon passed. It was Gandhini, the man from whom Tom had received the magic bottle, the one that would make him able to speak.

"Hop on!" he said, patting the wooden seat. Gandhini expected that Tom would have used the bottle he was given and was now eager to hear his story. Gandhini also hoped that Tom would have information about the state of the country, as he had heard many stories of unrest and several attacks by cabras. He had even heard tales of ugly, evil trolls.

"Sure," said Gecko from inside the armour, and Tom hopped up, glad to meet the friendly man once again. Gandhini assumed that Tom had used the bottle he was given, given that Tom responded. Gecko, still hidden, felt compelled to reveal who was actually speaking. He stepped out through the visor and introduced himself.

Gandhini had heard of the Limberik people but had never seen them. He was eager to learn everything about them, and his questions seemed almost endless. Gecko relished the opportunity to tell his story, and they didn't even notice as they approached the city gates.

The blue gate bore a large emblem, a white circle with a blue elephant. It had been a long time since the city had any elephants, but the symbol had remained, and it was very beautiful. Some thought the elephant slightly resembled the king, but that was a topic one had to be careful about discussing.
"You can stay over at my place. It's not a big house, but you should fit in," said Gandhini.

Both Gecko and Tom thought this was a good idea. Gecko looked back, but couldn't see if Art had followed them. Art should have seen them getting on the wagon, and they hoped he would understand that they had found lodging for the night in the city.
The two guards at the gate glanced at Sir Notalot. They did not recognise the emblem on his chest. Tom remained motionless.
"No worries," said Gandhini. "It's for sale," he said, removing Tom's helmet to show that it was just an empty suit of armour.
"Ten gold coins!" continued Gandhini. This was more than double what a suit of armour usually cost, and the guards shook their heads as they passed through the gate

and entered a high passage. The clatter of the ox's hooves echoed against the cobblestones.

Gandhini explained that the guards had become more vigilant recently. Many strange creatures had appeared around the city. He himself had been attacked along with Tom not so long ago.

The houses in the city were closely packed; Gandhini's wagon barely fit on the street. The sun-bleached facades were painted in all sorts of colours: yellow, green, red, blue. The simple wooden doors were low and wide. The houses were so narrow that there was usually only one small window per floor. But this single window was lavishly decorated with wooden balcony boxes and beautiful flowers.

Further into the city, the houses ended on one side, and they passed a wall instead. It was too high to see over, even from their elevated position on the cart.

"Here lives King Alberath," said Gandhini. "He lives in a palace behind a high wall in a city that is surrounded by a wall. The king also locks himself in at night when he goes to sleep."

"It sounds like your king is afraid of something?" wondered Gecko.

"Perhaps that happens when one believes oneself to be more than others, thinking one is more valuable," replied Gandhini. "His son's fiancée was kidnapped once, and such things can also make a king anxious."

After passing along the dark wall, which eventually came to an end, they entered a street lined with more colourful houses. Gandhini stopped in front of a narrow, light blue two-story house, which had a hoist on the second floor for loading goods."Here's my place!" he announced, and then asked the two to help unload.
Gandhini was a merchant, buying and selling almost anything people might need or not need. He often traveled to Larchville by the sea, sometimes to buy, sometimes to sell, often both. The small box of glass bottles he had traded with a wizard a long time ago. He often took the box with him on his business trips, but it was hard to find buyers for it, as everyone thought it was a hoax. The bottles had strange labels like "See," "Feel," "Rest," "Listen," "Silence." Gandhini had not used any of the bottles and did not know if they worked. He was surprised that Tom had not used the bottle on himself but had poured the magical liquid on a friend. Now he couldn't find out whether it worked or not.

Gandhini's house was not large. The hall was full of wooden crates, so the day's cargo had to be hoisted up to the second floor. They arranged the boxes in a row to form a bed for Gecko and Tom. Gandhini went into the kitchen, and soon the house was filled with the aroma of cooking. Gandhini, who sometimes traveled far, had collected many exciting spices. Celery, thyme, and basilica were all new to Tom and Gecko. They were served grilled cheese with various vegetables. There were many tasty sauces to accompany it, some spicy, some sweet, and all very delicious.

After the delicious meal, they all sat down on the floor. Gecko began to tell the story of the cave where he had lived as a child, located by the sea. Sometimes during storms, he and all his siblings had to squeeze together on a small shelf near the cave ceiling. Once, a wave pushed up to the ledge, and Gecko recounted how he fell into the water. He and the wave disappeared far down, and everyone screamed, thinking he would drown. But then the wave came up again, and Gecko hopped back onto the shelf, much to everyone's delight. It was perhaps this incident that turned Gecko into an adventurer.

From a distance, Art saw Sir Notalot getting on the wagon. He recognised the wagon and remembered that Tom had ridden in it once before. That time, Gecko wasn't there, and Tom couldn't speak. Now, perhaps they could sort out a thing or two.
Art walked alongside the road, a bit into the forest. The wagon moved slowly, and he had no trouble keeping up. He could hear them talking, but couldn't make out what they were saying. As they neared the city, when the wagon turned into the city, Art stopped and wondered what the two had planned to do now. Hidden in a thicket, he watched them. It didn't seem like they made any attempt to get off. Feeling a bit sad, Art watched from a distance as the carriage disappeared through the city gates.

As darkness fell, Art suspected that Tom and Gecko would likely stay inside the city for the night. Having lived a hundred years in solitude, he had never felt particularly lonely, but now he suddenly felt very abandoned. He told himself it was just for one night.

Art walked away from the city walls to find somewhere to spend the night. Day and night, there were always people moving around near the city, and he wanted to go a good distance away to be able to sleep undisturbed. He wandered for a long time, worried he might have trouble waking up in time to get back before the others left the city.

The darkness had deepened when strange noises, a mix of voices and perhaps animal sounds, reached his ears from ahead. He crept closer with caution. In a clearing, he glimpsed creatures and quickly took cover behind a tree to listen. Muffled conversations were underway, though the words remained indistinct to him. A little further, fires flickered to life, revealing a scene unlike any he had seen before. They were not humans. The clearing teemed with gnomes and cabras, their numbers reaching several hundred. Large trolls, brandishing whips and tools, laboured to keep order. Hidden in the shadows, Art watched, puzzled and intrigued, wondering what had brought this diverse assembly together in the depths of the forest.

He crept even closer because he wanted to hear what the trolls were talking about.

"We'll wait here until the others arrive," grunted a large troll named Joorgh.

No, we attack now and take all the loot for ourselves," argued Clouss, the smaller troll with red stripey hair, 'smaller' might be a misnomer, as Clouss was larger than Art, but for a troll, Clouss was not particularly large.

"We don't stand a chance of taking the city with just a few hundred cabras, we must wait for the others." The latest voice came from near Art. It was Mozta, the large troll sitting not far from Art's hiding place. He hadn't initially seen her because trolls are difficult to spot in a dark forest. This was uncomfortably close, and Art froze, holding his breath.

The first troll continued, "Tomorrow, the others will come, lots of trolls, thousands of gnomes, and even more cabras. Then we will attack, and not before. Is that understood?"

Art was horrified; this could not happen. He needed to do something. He thought of Tom and Gecko; he had to warn them. He had to warn everyone in the city.

Art listened further, not daring to move, and then heard that all the beasts were coming from a hole in the ground near Wyrmville. Art immediately thought of his nightmares; the recurring black hole was not a dream, but reality. The mountain, Heart, had left behind a hole to the underworld, and it was from this hole that all the trolls, gnomes, and other creatures were emerging. "We need to get Heart back in her place," Art thought, deciding to head to the city right away.

He looked back, but saw nothing, not the ground, no trees, it was completely dark. When he had crept up to the tree, it had been lighter, but now everything around him was pitch black. He tried to turn around, but it was impossible; the turning radius of a dragon is very large. Moreover, he had a large troll just a few meters beside him. He had to back up.
But backing up with a long tail pointing straight back is not easy. He tried to look between his legs, but his tail got stuck between two trees and a branch broke off with a crash. Art stopped abruptly, everything was silent.
He slowly lifted his gaze and looked into the faces of three wide-eyed trolls staring back at him, gaping. Then everything happened very fast, Clouss lunged at Art, grabbing him tightly around the neck so that Art couldn't breathe fire. The other two trolls grabbed his legs and started dragging the dragon into the centre of the clearing.

Trolls hated dragons, cabras hated dragons, it seemed like everyone who had gathered that night hated dragons. Dragons were the worst thing they knew. They all thought it was the dragons' fault that all trolls, gnomes, and other creatures were once banished to the underworld. Capturing a dragon was worth much more than conquering the city. Everyone cheered as Art was dragged forward. He was tied to a tree and subjected to both spit

and mockery. They tied his mouth so he could neither speak nor breathe fire.
"The dragon must die!" roared the crowd.
"We'll eat him up," screeched others.
Mozta stepped in front of the dragon.
"No!" she bellowed. "First, we will show the dragon to the others, then we will eat it," she chuckled.
The dragon was to be shown alive to the great army that was on its way. What a tribute this would be for the trolls. Mozta also wanted to personally present the dragon to Mephistor, the ruler of the underworld. The cruel warlord was due to arrive tomorrow, and the captured dragon would elevate Mozta's status. This looked very promising for her.

With the dragon tied up in the middle, it became easier for the trolls to keep the cabra horde in order. They had something else to argue about, something new to focus on.
The trolls' feast continued deep into the night. Art tried to break free, but it was utterly impossible. Tomorrow, he would be forced to watch an army of trolls, gnomes, and cabras lay siege to the city, if he even lived that long.

It was a beautiful morning in Hagriven. The sun's rays sought their way over the walls and began to warm the stone houses. No one could suspect that in a few hours, the city would be surrounded and in the midst of war.
Sir Notalot and Gecko set off early, both feeling a bit guilty for having left Art alone in the forest overnight.

Gandhini also joined them, eager to meet the dragon. A dragon was something he had never seen before, even though he had been close the first time he met Tom. He had even briefly spoken with Art without realising it. Gandhini found the prospect of getting to know the dragon very exciting.

They left Gandhini's house on foot, not needing a wagon. Approaching the gatekeeper, Gecko worried there might be trouble, as it had been an empty suit of armour the day before when they arrived.
Gandhini greeted the guard with a good morning and then mentioned he had been forced to sell the armour at a very low price. The guard laughed, noting that it was always the case when Gandhini sold something. Tom gave a thumbs up, appearing as a very satisfied customer.

They all expected to find Art standing by the road outside the city waiting for them. But Art was not there. They went back to the place where they had left him, but he wasn't there either. They called out, but there was no answer.
"Maybe he followed the road past the city?" Gecko suggested. "That's where we're heading."

They turned around. They continued to look and call out, even though they had just walked the same stretch. It felt as if he could appear at any moment, yet he was nowhere to be found. They walked all the way back, continued around and past the city, but no dragon was to be found.

The trolls danced around Art, poking him with sticks and spears as if to check if he was tender enough. They laughed and mocked the dragon, calling him names like frog and chameleon. The taunting had gone on almost all night. Art feared that soon the great army would arrive, and then it would be the end for him, his friends, and perhaps the entire city.

Despite all the noise, Art could distinguish a faint thudding in the ground, a deeper thud than the trolls' dancing. Art realised that Heart was on her way. At first, he felt relieved, hoping to be saved, but then he began to wonder what the mountain could do for him in his predicament. Why would she care about him? She might just laugh at him too.

After a while, even the trolls heard the heavy footsteps and fell silent. They didn't understand what they were hearing. They looked in all directions but saw nothing; everything was dark. Then, suddenly, a massive cliff wall appeared in the light of the fires.

A mountain was moving along the entire camp. The herd scattered, some cabras getting crushed under the mountain's advance. The trolls swung their whips in the air to prevent the creatures from fleeing, but it was futile. The trolls also felt terror at the sight of the mountain. One side of the cliff wall lifted high into the air and landed on Mozta. She screamed and tried to jump away but was crushed under Heart's immense weight. The other trolls attempted to run, but Heart quickly caught up and

squashed one of them. Terrified, all the cabras dispersed, running in every direction. Heart tried to follow, but she couldn't move quickly enough. After a short while, she was back by Art.
"Thousand blasting rocks, what nasty creatures," she muttered, looking down at Art. "I can't untie you, but I can guard you so no beasts can harm you. Where are the rest of your companions?"
Art nodded his snout towards the city.

Gandhini noticed something unusual in the distant landscape. A hill, far off in the horizon, caught his attention - one he didn't recognise. Tom and Gecko, grasping the potential significance of this, instantly understood what it might be. Without hesitation, Tom broke into a run towards it, with Gandhini quickly following suit.
"Heart," yelled Gecko. "It's Heart, Art must be there."

As they approached, they saw the mountain standing amidst an area of fallen trees. Both Tom and Gecko wondered why she had done it this way. Then they discovered all the flattened beasts and trolls among the crushed trees. In the midst of all this stood Art with a bandage around his mouth, tied to a tree. Gecko ran forward, jumped up on Art's shoulder, and began untying the mouth bandage. Art immediately started yelling and screaming about the terrible night he had had. Gecko crawled around the tree and released his arms.

Gandhini approached the scene and Art fell silent. He recognised the man who had left with Tom, but he did not know him. Could he trust the man? Gecko understood that Art felt discomfort and pointed out that it was okay, Gandhini is decent, he's helping us.

Art knew he had to warn the town somehow, he couldn't do it alone. Gandhini would make a very good messenger. Art recounted how he had been ambushed by trolls and goblins during the night.

"There is a large herd of goblins and cabras not far from here. Terrible trolls have the command and they are waiting for thousands more to arrive during the day," Tom looked around in all directions, he seemed very scared, while Art continued his account. "They are planning a major attack," he said, turning to Gandhini.

"You must go back and warn the city immediately," continued Art. "Prepare the city for the worst battle you can imagine. These enemies are not to be taken lightly. They were the ones who attacked me and tied me up," Art said, gesticulating so intensely that Gandhini stepped back.

"You must stay and help us," pleaded Gandhini.

"We can't be on the battlefield, we would only scare your soldiers," explained Art. "We are on our way to the coast, we have another important errand."

"But," interrupted Gecko. "I think we should stay and help."

"No," Art replied firmly. "These trolls and monstrosities come from the underworld, from a hole that formed when the mountain tore itself away and began searching for us.

More and more beasts are coming all the time; we must stop this by putting the mountain back in its place. That will be our task in this war."
Gandhini understood the importance of warning everyone and preparing the city for the impending attack. He said goodbye and hurriedly walked back towards Hagriven.
The dragon, Sir Notalot, Gecko, and Heart set off on the final leg of their journey, towards the Dawnfall Castle. They must find out how, in some way, to transform the mountain back into a mountain again.
The path they were walking on was overgrown in places. Trade between the castle and the other cities along the coast was mostly by sea. It was very rare for anyone to walk this road. Sometimes, they would lose the path as it was hard to see in the vegetation.
But they all agreed on one thing. After this journey, there would be no problem finding the path. Heart was actually levelling the path and significantly widening it. They were walking on a path that was hard to find, but leaving behind a main road that could have been seen from the moon.

In the evening, after the first day's journey, they arrived at a small lake. The land they had reached was called Dinghli, a land Gecko referred to as dreadful because of its vegetation.
It had already darkened when they decided to stay overnight. They had been walking slowly all day. There was no point in going faster because they would still have to wait for Heart when they reached the coast. No more

cabras had been seen during the day. They didn't know what this meant; perhaps none were moving in this part of the country.

It could also mean that Tom and the mountain had scared them, kept them at a distance. What was clear was that these underworld beasts were very afraid of Tom and they also shied away from Heart. Perhaps the magical liquid that both had been soaked in had a frightening effect on the beasts from the underworld.

Chapter 16:

Dawnfall Castle

It was the seagulls that were their first contact with the coast. The stream they had followed from the lake during the day had now grown into a small river. They hadn't met any people, which was good, as a wandering mountain and a dragon attract a lot of attention and it was hard to hide in the open landscape.
Later in the day, they came to a cliff where the river threw itself into the air. Art called to Heart to stay where she was while the others sneaked up to the edge to scout. Below them was a large plateau, this land was called Dawnfall, just like the castle. Beyond this was another steep cliff plunging into the sea.

In the mist from the waterfall, they saw a tall castle with a moat filled by the river that had gathered again after falling over the edge. The castle was white with delicate high towers. The blue roofs were lofty and pointed. The Dinger river now flowed on either side of the high wall that ran around the entire castle. The castle's drawbridge was lowered but the gate was closed.

The entire plateau around the castle was cultivated, and small farms were scattered like little white flowers on a meadow.

"There's the castle!" said Art, turning to Gecko.
"We'll do as we planned, you two go down and talk to them. I probably shouldn't show myself," said Art and went back to Heart to tell her about the plan.

It turned out to be too steep to go directly down to the plateau. Tom and Gecko had to take a long detour to find a descent. The path they followed was sloping and wound down the cliff away from the castle.
Once down, the road changed direction and went straight back towards the castle. They passed many farms, and the people they met greeted the lone knight in armour politely.
Together, they had thought about what to say when they arrived. Still, they were nervous as they approached the drawbridge.
The gates were still closed, and Tom looked up. On the wall stood two guards, one of whom called out to them.
"Halt! What do you want?"
"I am looking for the owner of this armour," replied Gecko from inside the helmet of Sir Notalot.
There was silence for a moment, then both guards started to laugh.
"You're asking us about who owns your armour?"
Gecko realised he had phrased the question a bit oddly.
"I mean I am looking for the previous owner of this armour."
The other guard then noticed the emblem on Tom's chest and whispered to his colleague.
"It looks like Prince Robert's old armour."

The first guard didn't like this development, as such a scenario was not described in the instruction manual for the bridge guard. After carefully considering all possibilities, he shouted loudly, despite the other guard standing right next to him.
"Fetch Prince Robert Wenchester."
The other guard immediately ran off. Tom and Gecko looked nervously up towards the mountain where Art was waiting. The mountain was not visible, but they knew she and Art were up there.
A young man with long light hair stepped forward on the wall.
"What do you want from me?"
"Do you recognise me?" asked Gecko.
The Prince looked surprised at his old armour. He hadn't expected to see it again. Who had found it and what did they want? Robert began to suspect that it was people from the village near the Mount Dragon who wanted to blame him for the village's destruction shortly after his visit.
"It's not my fault the village was destroyed. If you settle so close to a terrible dragon, you have only yourself to blame. Go away, you can keep the armour but leave us in peace," said Prince Robert and disappeared from the wall.
"But that's not what we meant," replied Gecko, but it was too late.
"You heard him, get out of here," roared the guard.
Tom and Gecko were tired and sad when they returned to Art and Heart. Art saw from a distance that they had failed and asked.

"Isn't he there?"
"Yes, the prince is in the castle, and it is indeed his armour, but he doesn't want to talk to us."
"Why doesn't he want to talk?"
Heart came closer and heard what they were talking about. She reacted strongly, as usual, and roared.
"I will turn the castle into a gravel pit."
Art quickly understood that this was not the right approach.
"No, we should not destroy anything. Sit down and let us think."
The mountain stopped, right in the middle of the river. For her, the waterways were just small puddles, and she didn't think small thoughts. Wherever she stopped, something was crushed or destroyed; she no longer cared about such things.
"The prince thinks we come from Wyrmville and blames him for the destruction of the village," explained Gecko. "He refuses to talk to us from now on."
"What do we do now?" Art pondered, looking out over the landscape. The river was dried up, and the waterfall had quieted. Art looked around and saw that Heart was sitting right in the river.
"Hey, Heart, you've dammed the river, move, carefully."
The mountain moved very cautiously to the side so that the water could slowly return to its original level. Silently, they watched as the water once again plunged over the edge.
"I've got an idea," said Art.

Tom and Gecko approached the castle a second time. The guard had seen the knight walking towards the castle for a long time and had plenty of time to think about what he would say.

"Get out of here, we are done talking to you," said the guard emphatically. Then he thought the knight would turn around and never come back. Unfortunately, it didn't go that way, and Gecko replied firmly.

"But we have not finished talking to you. We want to speak with Prince Robert again."

The guard was very surprised by the answer.

"We?"

Prince Robert had been standing in the background and stepped forward when he realised that the guard would not succeed in driving away the uninvited guest.

"If you don't stop disturbing us immediately, we will have you imprisoned."

Sir Notalot then slowly lifted his right arm, as a stop sign. After a short while, everything went silent, the waterfall was gone. Tom had signalled to Art, who in turn called to Heart to create a dam by sitting in the river.

Prince Robert looked in surprise at the sinking water level, then up at the waterfall, and saw only cliffs, a dried-up waterfall. He looked in horror at his old armour. Tom lowered his arm and Gecko shouted.

"I just want you to answer a few questions about this armour. If you don't answer, I will flood the castle."

Without a change in expression, Prince Robert turned to his guards.

"Put him in the prison."

The guards disappeared and after a long while, the gate slowly opened. Tom waved his arms and Gecko thought of something that would sound like a spell.
"Dosla voda dosla," yelled Gecko, and Tom waved his arms in rhythm.
Art saw Tom's gesticulation and called to the mountain to release the water, this time Art wanted all the water to come at once.

Sir Notalot turned around and hurried away from the castle. The guards who had opened the gate watched the knight walk away and thought that the mission was completed. They closed the gate and happily returned to the prince up on the wall.

The water came out over the waterfall with full force, and a cascade of water then filled the entire castle. Tom turned around again and calmly walked up to the castle as the water receded. A soaking wet Wenchester climbed up on the wall and stuck his head out again.
"Okay, it was me who tricked the dragon. What do you want me to do about this?"
The princess, who was named Esterella, had now come up on the wall and recognised the armour that the prince had used when she was freed. Tom had not seen her before and did not react when she waved at him.

The first part of the mission was thus completed, and Tom started waving for Art to come down to them. The dragon misunderstood this and asked the mountain to dam up the

river again. Everyone now looked terrified as the water disappeared again and understood what would happen next.
"No, not that again!" yelled Gecko, seeing no other solution than to run up to Art and Heart to stop this powerful variation in the water level.
He jumped out of the armour, through the visor, and started running along the road. Tom was not quite up to speed with the rapid sequence of events and lost his balance, falling backwards.
What Wenchester and the guards saw was an armour collapsing as a very small person jumped out of it, much too small for the armour. The fact that the person had also left the armour through the visor did not make things any better.
They couldn't believe their eyes, dropped their jaws, and looked generally foolish. It didn't get any better when Tom finally stood up.

Robert Wenchester now began to suspect that the armour was still the empty armour that he had once brought to life. However, he had never seen a Limberik before and could not understand the connection between his old armour and the small creature. The guards were harder to convince, and they probably still believe to this day that it was a very small man in a much too big armour.

It was not fast for Gecko to go up the hill. It took time to run as he had to take detours around the smallest hole and stone. When he arrived at the top, he saw the dragon and the mountain and began to wave his arms. Art saw him coming and understood that something had gone wrong. When Gecko arrived and explained what had happened, Heart slowly began to release the water. Gradually, it lifted itself so that the water once again cascaded over the edge, just as it always had. Everyone at the castle looked up at the waterfall, which was slowly increasing in strength.

This time the water did not come as quickly. From the height, they could see the ground rising, a mountain walking. The mountain stopped at the edge, and everyone could then see that on top of the mountain sat a dragon. Gecko was also there, but he was not visible from the long distance. Then the princess peered out from behind the prince.
"Look, there's my dragon!"

The dragon would have preferred not to show itself, but Heart and Gecko persuaded him. Art was ashamed of what he had done when he was here before, when he had kidnapped the princess and locked her in his cave. He now realised that it was very selfish of him. He would have preferred to wait at a distance and then hear what the others had decided.
But the mountain thought differently and offered the dragon a seat. Riding on a mountain is a privilege few have, and the dragon could not refuse such an offer. At the same time, he was a bit curious and impressed by the man who had managed to trick him and then free the princess.

He began to think that it would be nice to meet the princess again. He had never been explicitly unkind to her, at least not in his own view. However, he had placed her alone in a cage, inside a cave. Gradually, Art began to realise that this might not have been such a good idea. All had gathered on the plateau above the castle. It was the only place that worked since the mountain insisted on being part of the meeting. The mountain couldn't descend to the plateau below, as it was too steep.
Prince Robert and Princess Esterella were there, along with Gecko, Art, and the old armour. Some significant people from the castle were also present. They were there, of course, with the desire to feel more important than they were.

Art recounted what had happened after the prince and princess left the cave. He spoke of how he thought his treasure chamber was invaded by warriors and how he defended it against the intruders.
Art described the hole that had formed after the mountain moved and the terrible creatures that emerged from it. How they had now spread across almost the entire world. He also showed how Art and Sir Notalot had become good friends and how they were accused of attacking Wyrmville.
Gecko then continued and talked about how he met his friends and about the castle with the dragon queen. Many in the group were amazed by the story of the dragon queen. Having recently seen their first dragon and then

hearing about a dragon queen was almost too much for them.

Prince Wenchester then told the story of how he had set off for Wyrmville in an attempt to somehow rescue the princess, without a concrete plan in mind. On his way to Wyrmville, he stayed overnight in Marlock, a day's journey up the coast. There, he met Merglan, an old wizard. The man told him about the magical bottles in the dragon's cave and how they could be used to trick the dragon. He was to look for a discreet wooden box.
“The box would contain several bottles, and I was only to use the one labeled 'Animate',” the prince explained.
Art interrupted him.
“I remember that ugly chest, but I never bothered to open it. Are you saying there were more bottles, one of which could reverse what the first one did?”
Prince Robert nodded. “On one of the bottles, it was written 'Deanimate'. The chest was to the right as you entered the main hall.”
“And you left the other bottles there?”
Prince Robert continued nodding.
“The chest must still be intact, for had it broken, the mountain would have solidified and become an ordinary mountain again," said the dragon, pointing at the mountain. "And there are other things within the chest, items of great power and significance. Had they been unleashed, even more dreadful events could have occurred. Heart then began to gnash its teeth frantically.

The dragon quickly understood what the mountain was trying to do – it wanted to crush the bottles still inside it. "Wait, not here, you can't become a mountain in this place! We can't move you. You must first return to your place near Wyrmville and block the hole to the underworld."

Art also thought about the other magical bottles in the chest. Who knew what they could do to the mountain? He turned to Gecko.
"You'll have to go in and retrieve the bottle before it breaks," he said. "You're the only one who can slip in and find a way into the mountain."
Gecko was quick to agree. He had fantasised about the treasure that was said to be in the mountain and found the prospect exciting.
"Sure, miner Gecko is on it," he said, hopping towards the mountain to begin his operation. Armed with a small burning torch, he approached Heart, which hesitantly opened its mouth.

Deep within the mountain, Gecko encountered a realm of dense stone. He had to navigate carefully, crawling under large boulders and squeezing through tight gaps. Occasionally, he found small openings that allowed him to venture further, but more often, he reached dead ends, blocked by the mountain's impenetrable Heart.
Initially, it seemed there was nothing but stone. Disheartenment crept in as Gecko started to doubt the existence of any treasure or the sought-after bottle.

Pushing himself under a massive stone block, he emerged on the other side to a surprising glimmer in the gravel. Scattered gold coins lay before him. He set his torch down, picked up a coin, contemplating whether to leave with this minor find.
However, the thought of returning with just a coin while a magical bottle was expected spurred him on. Deeper into the mountain, the treasure grew: gold coins, precious stones, golden pitchers, silver jewellery, gold necklaces, and emeralds. The riches were immense, tempting him to abandon his quest for the bottle and take the gold instead. Yet, the chest was nowhere to be seen. A collapsed chamber blocked by huge stone blocks thwarted his search. Gecko had no choice but to retreat. Outside, he appealed to the mountain, asking it to rearrange its insides to reveal the chest. The mountain rumbled in response, its interior churning as stones and blocks shifted, creating new passages.
On his second attempt, Gecko discovered the chest amid the sea of gold. It was damaged, but the bottles inside appeared intact. He tried to pull out the entire chest, but it was too heavy and crumbled under his efforts. The lid was easy to remove, and Gecko peered inside with amazement. Among the bottles was one labeled "Deanimate," much larger than he had anticipated. He struggled to move it, shuffling gold coins in front and behind the bottle to gradually inch it forward.
The process was slow, and those waiting outside grew anxious. "Has he become trapped?" they wondered. "He's moving in there," the mountain reassured softly. To

Gecko, the mountain's rumbling felt like an earthquake, sparking fear that the bottle might break. But the tremors had opened a new path, allowing Gecko to drag the bottle the final distance.
Art was the first to see Gecko emerge. "Here he comes!" he shouted joyously, reaching in to help with the bottle. Together, they pulled out both Gecko and the bottle.
"We have the bottle!" Art exclaimed, holding it aloft triumphantly.
Gecko, still eyeing the gold, tried to dart back into the mountain's mouth to snatch some of the treasure, but Heart quickly closed its mouth. It was an adventure that would become a legendary tale, one that would outlast any gold. Gecko consoled himself with this thought, realising the story of their daring endeavour would be treasured for generations to come.

Finally, they had secured the bottle, and a wave of applause rippled through the group, a collective expression of delight that this phase of their mission was accomplished. Art thought he saw branches on the mountain's slope moving as if clapping – it almost seemed as if the mountain itself was applauding their success. However, their moment of jubilation was abruptly cut short. From the other side of the mountain, roars and screams erupted, shattering the brief peace. Suddenly, an army of trolls, goblins, cabras, and other monstrous creatures swarmed around Heart the mountain. They clambered over each other in a frenzied rush; trolls shoved cabras aside in their eagerness to lead the charge.

The ground quivered under the thunderous stampede of thousands of feet. The mountain had masked the sound of the approaching army, and everyone's attention had been so fixated on Gecko's endeavour that they hadn't noticed an entire army sneaking up on them.
They quickly realised they needed to retreat to the castle. The group began sprinting towards the path that led down to the plateau. The mountain itself transformed into a protective barrier, shielding the fleeing party. The monstrous horde swarmed everywhere, yet they never ventured up the mountain. Heart shielded them until they reached the road, but she couldn't follow them down to the plateau. However, it successfully prevented any trolls or cabras from pursuing them.

As they made their hurried descent, the sounds of the chaotic battle above echoed behind them. The urgency of their mission had just become even more apparent – they needed to restore the mountain, and quickly, not only for their sake but also to stem the tide of creatures threatening their world.

As the attackers dispersed, they filled the entire edge of the plateau, except where the mountain stood as a sentinel. Art paused and looked up, witnessing trolls, goblins, and cabras crowding around the waterfall and stretching as far as his eyes could see in the other direction. Glancing down at the castle, he couldn't imagine how such a modest stronghold could withstand these enemies once they descended onto the plain. It was

a matter of time before they would come down, sooner or later.
On the other side of the plateau, the landscape sloped downwards, and it was here that the monsters began to advance onto the plain in front of the castle. Art hurried onward, hoping they could reach the castle before the next wave of assault.
Upon reaching the lowlands, Prince Robert Wenchester sprinted towards the farms to alert the inhabitants. "Get to the castle immediately, we are under attack!" he shouted. Princess Esterella did the same, and soon they were all spread across the field, alerting everyone as the attackers made their descent onto the plain far behind them. "Leave everything and run to the castle," Esterella yelled.
Some people ran out of their farms only to see the dragon and, terrified, ran back inside. The prince had to persuade them to leave their homes and flee to the castle, for something far worse was approaching. As they conveyed the urgency, the peasants began to understand the gravity of the situation. Families gathered their loved ones, abandoning their homes and possessions, driven by the fear of the looming threat.
The sight of the castle's gates opening to welcome the flood of villagers was a poignant reminder of the impending danger. As the last of the villagers hurried inside, the castle's defenders prepared for what was to come, bolstering the gates and fortifying their defences. The air was tense with anticipation, a stark contrast to the usually peaceful lowlands, now transformed into a battlefield against an otherworldly threat.

Art tried to stay out of the way to avoid delaying the evacuation. The farms closest to the castle had already noticed the commotion and were rushing to seek shelter. Now, Art, along with Sir Notalot and Gecko, were running at the back of the group. As Art looked back, he saw the entire plateau behind him swarming with creatures. Some cabras even ran alongside them. High on the ridge, Heart stood, but all it could do was prevent the enemy from descending along the road.

The officials from the meeting seemed to think they had priority access to the castle, followed by the population who hurried in after them. The prince and princess assisted, ensuring everyone's safety. Suddenly, a cabras lunged forward, striking Princess Esterella and knocking her to the ground. Tom quickly rushed to her aid, his bare armour intimidating enough to scare off the beast. Esterella was unharmed and hurried towards the gates. Soon, everyone would be safe, at least for a little while. The castle gates closed just as the last of the villagers and their rescuers crossed the threshold. The thuds and roars of the creatures outside echoed against the stone walls, a grim reminder of the siege they were now under. Inside the castle, there was a sense of relief mixed with fear; they were safe for now, but for how long? Outside, the monstrous horde prowled, searching for any weakness in the castle's defences.

The sense of urgency was palpable as everyone inside the castle prepared for what might come next. The defenders took their positions, archers readied their bows, and the castle's inhabitants braced themselves. Art, Tom, and Gecko, despite their exhaustion, knew they had a crucial role to play in the defence of the castle and the eventual counterattack. They exchanged determined looks, ready to stand together against whatever lay ahead.

Tom, Gecko, and the prince formed a protective barrier, ensuring that everyone had time to enter the castle safely. The creatures, avoiding Tom, ran around him. Tom tried to be everywhere at once, but it was of no use; the number of creatures only seemed to increase.
The prince cut his way to the drawbridge, calling out to Tom and Art with urgency, "Come, hurry!" Now, everyone was safe inside the castle, except for Tom and the dragon, who stood like a small island amidst the sea of monstrous beings.

The menacing chants of the trolls circling them, shouting "Kill the dragon," filled the air.
They made their way to the drawbridge and began to back up onto it. The soldiers in the castle immediately started to wind up the drawbridge, causing the dragon and the armour to roll through the castle gate. The massive gate was quickly shut behind them, sealing off the castle from the horde outside.

The archers on the wall shot arrows into the mass on the other side of the moat, but it made no difference. The castle was now surrounded and the trolls threw themselves into the moat so that cabras and other beasts could run over them. The trolls then leaned against the wall so that the others could climb up.

On the wall, they met substantial resistance. The soldiers of Dawnfall Castle might not have experienced a war in their lifetimes, but they were well-trained and strong. They could fight. As soon as a cabras made it up the wall, it was surrounded by five soldiers, all very skilled swordsmen. But a cabras is not killed with a single blow; it takes many well-aimed strikes before it falls to the ground.

Heart could not do much from the height. She stamped on the edge and managed to cause a landslide that almost took her down too. The landslide swept across the plateau, destroying many farms and burying a mass of enemies.

Those who escaped were instead washed into the sea. In vain, the trolls clung to the boulders that slowly twisted around before disappearing into the foaming water. The landslide halted the advancing army, but only for a short while. As soon as the landslide stopped, the monsters jumped over the debris and ran towards the castle.

Tom ran on the ridge, scaring away goblins attempting to cross the wall, but as soon as he left a place, they were there again. Art spewed fire and could confuse the cabras so that the soldiers could attack with their well-placed strikes.

For a while, it seemed as though they could hold out, but more and more invaders kept coming up on the wall. It was impossible to keep them at bay and the soldiers began to retreat.

Down in the courtyard, things were no better; some goblins had already entered and were now working to open the gates and lower the drawbridge.
It seemed they would not be able to hold the castle much longer. In the midst of the enemy army, a red figure wrapped in black mist floated slowly towards the castle. All the beasts bowed and threw themselves to the ground before the creature. Dawnfall's archers shot a volley of arrows, but they just bounced off the figure. In the black smoke, lightning wandered, cracking and sparkling, and occasionally a bolt flew off and killed any beast in its way.
The trolls cheered and screamed.
"Mephistor! Mephistor!"

Chapter 17:

Gandhini Plays the Theatre

Gandhini had hurried back to the city of Hagriven to warn everyone about the attack that Art had spoken of. He saw the white city from a distance and thought about what was to come. He felt how much he loved his hometown.
He thought about all the people who, unknowingly, had recently started their daily routines. The sun was shining, the birds were chirping, would they really believe him? A simple merchant telling tales of trolls and goblins.
Most had never seen such creatures, many were entirely sure they did not exist. How could he be credible?
He stopped and pondered. He must bring proof. He turned around and hoped that Art and the others would still be there to help him find something.
Unfortunately, Art and his group had already left when Gandhini returned to the scene. The ground was flattened by the devastation of the mountain. He could find a few flattened trolls, but he saw nothing that he could use to support his story.
He knelt down and began to sift through the remains of a troll, hoping to find something.

After a while of searching, he found three large rings that had been attached to what looked like an ear. Not much for evidence, he thought, but he put them in his pocket anyway. He found a couple of ornate rings, which were around a loose finger. He removed these, but quickly realised that they were not suitable as evidence. Such cheap rings could be bought anywhere. He was about to stand up when he heard voices.

A couple of goblins were walking straight towards him, but they had not yet discovered him. They were poking around in the ground. Asbrak was the name of the larger one, big for a wight, but not as tall as a full-grown human. His companion was named Kas, they had come to see if there was anything of value among the dead.
"It's just trash, I tell you," said Asbrak. He wore a torn gray cloak and was not much taller than the kneeling Gandhini.
"But we might find something valuable, trolls usually have rings and necklaces," said Kas. He limped a bit, one leg was crooked and made him appear shorter than he actually was. They began to rummage in the remains of the troll.
"Ah, these rings are usually not gold, just trash, trolls like trash," said Asbrak, who did not like trolls.

Gandhini realised that he would be discovered at any moment. Better to nip it in the bud, he thought, and pulled his cloak in front of him while already kneeling. He dragged some cloth scraps from the troll over his feet. At the same time, he picked up some dirt and smeared it into his face.

"I have some fine gold rings that I'm willing to trade," said Gandhini without standing up.

The goblins stopped and stared at the strange creature. In the underworld, there are many peculiar beings; one can look pretty much however they want.
This peculiar form of liberalism led the goblins to take Gandhini for one of their own. Goblins thought humans were ugly, but they also thought goblins were ugly, not to mention trolls. The creature before them was too short to be human, so it must be a wight. An unusually ugly wight, he almost looked like a human in the face, thought Kas. Just another greedy wight trying to make a profit from the devastation. Besides, a human would never bargain with a wight.
"Sure, let's see what you've got." Asbrak's delight at making a good deal meant he also didn't scrutinise the man enough to discover the ruse.

Gandhini had the rings he found in his clenched right hand. He slowly unfolded his hand to make them look valuable.
Kas exclaimed, "Oh, it looks like gold."
Asbrak hit him and said curtly, "Nonsense, it's troll trash."
Gandhini closed his hand again. Asbrak licked his lips. "We can be generous and buy your rings. We have no money, but we have some clothes and a knife." Asbrak couldn't think of anything else valuable but added anyway, "We also have our wight candles, of course."

Wight candles are something all goblins have, so it was mostly meant as a joke.
"Your wight candles will do," said Gandhini quickly.
Asbrak tried to hide his joy and at the same time stopped Kas, who was about to bring out his candle.
"These are fine candles, barely used," said Asbrak. "We want more for our candles. Do you have anything else?"
Gandhini pulled out one of the rings he had found earlier. He realised he needed to haggle over the price, or else he would be forced to reveal everything he owned.
"You can have this ring too, but then I want your knife," he said.
The goblins then brought out their candles, which were enclosed in very small glass bottles. Gandhini received them while avoiding looking at the flame. Then he also got the knife. It was a clumsy, rusty iron knife with a thick back; Gandhini had never seen anything like it.
"Remember, we are soon marching east to slay the dragon," said Asbrak quickly, wanting to change the subject. He thought he had made a very good deal and was afraid that the seller would regret it when he saw the worthless knife.
Gandhini didn't know what to say. The goblins apparently knew that Art and his group had headed east, and now it seemed they were going to have a whole army on their heels. They would never manage on their own.
"But we were supposed to attack the city," said Gandhini, feeling compelled to say something.
"No, new orders, Mephistor has come to this world and the ruler wants us to kill the dragon first," said Asbrak,

saliva spraying from his mouth as he mentioned the prince's name.

Mephistor was the ruler of the underworld, an evil being who hated all living things. Few were the humans who had seen him, and he is described as a small man, reddish complexion, with horns and sparse black fur, like the bristles on a pig. It was said that humans could neither harm nor kill him, that only dragons could inflict damage on him. That's why he hated dragons more than anything. Mephistor had power over everyone in the underworld, possessing an invisible force that gave him the ability to control and command the subterranean masses.

Mephistor had now left his realm, and it was evident in the way the beasts no longer rampaged indiscriminately. Now they were gathered, now they were an army with a leader, now they could attack and destroy at will. Mephistor had ordered that the dragon be killed first of all, for once the last dragon was dead, he would be omnipotent. The invisible command spread among all the beasts, and with each passing hour, more and more gathered. Slowly they united into groups, waiting for a new order from the ruler.
"We kill the dragon first," said Gandhini, hoping the goblins would continue their search and leave him alone. He had heard of the ruler from the underworld but always thought it was just tales. Now, having seen all these strange creatures, he began to realise that Mephistor might very well exist. He must get to the city as quickly

as possible to warn the people and the king. Gandhini had not yet figured out how he could warn the dragon that they were being pursued and threatened. Could he make his way to the dragon unseen, while Mephistor had an entire army heading in the same direction?

One thing at a time, he must first get back to the city and warn the king. But the goblins didn't seem to want to leave him unsupervised. They suspected he was a trickster, one who didn't want to fight but stayed on the sidelines, scavenging from the dead.
"You'd better go back to your camp," Asbrak advised him.
"We'll search a bit more," Gandhini suggested, hoping for an opportunity to slip away. The two goblins said nothing and continued to poke around in the remains of the troll.

Gandhini looked around for a way to escape, but it seemed hopeless. From a distance, he noticed a troop of goblins and cabras accompanied by a large troll with a whip. The whole group was looking at the ground, trying to be as inconspicuous as possible to avoid the whip. The troll cracked the whip in the air and kept looking around, as if expecting a large audience to suddenly appear and admire him and his whip. Asbrak and Kas began to look around anxiously, apparently not wanting to be seen either. The troop was passing by the edge of the woods on their way east and would soon disappear from view.

"Asbrak and Kas! Come here at once!" The troll had spotted them and initially thought they were admiring his handling of the whip, but quickly realised who they were. Gandhini hoped this would present an opportunity to escape. But it could just as easily end with him being exposed. If the troll and the goblins came over, it was likely that one of them would notice he was a human kneeling down.
"You better go back. I'll fall in when my troop passes," said Gandhini, trying to sound convincing.

Asbrak and Kas shuffled off. They both knew that if they started arguing with the stranger, they would only get more harassed by the troop waiting for them.

Gandhini began to crawl away on his knees in the opposite direction. He lay on his stomach and crawled slowly. Every now and then, he looked over his shoulder to see how the two goblins were approaching the troop. Gandhini crawled next to a large stone and turned his face down into the ground. He lay completely still, hoping he wouldn't be noticed. When Asbrak reached the troop, he turned to look out over the field. He saw nothing of the strange wight and as he was about to open his mouth, he was ordered to be quiet and get in line.
"Forward!" bellowed the troll, still annoyed that there was no audience as he had thought, but just two dirty goblins. Gandhini started breathing again when he heard the command. He felt the vibrations in the ground as the group began marching again. He continued to crawl while

the troop marched in the opposite direction. Once he was out of sight, he stood up and ran as fast as he could.

In the city, Gandhini had no trouble getting in. No one in the city had any idea about the horrible creatures that had surrounded the city during the night. The guard at the gate let him in without any problems. Gandhini immediately ran to King Alberath's residence.
"Stop, you can't come in here," said the well-dressed guard at the gate. The guard was particular about who he dealt with. One must be humble, almost to the point of fawning, with a superior, but a regular townsfolk could be treated however one liked, and the guard took every chance to be unpleasant.
"I have a very important matter for King Alberath," said Gandhini quickly.
"Let's take it easy here," replied the guard slowly and clearly, as if talking to a child. He had been bullied by some officials visiting the king earlier in the morning and felt like getting back at someone in some way.

Gandhini, having no time for such foolishness, took out one of the wight candles. He held it up in front of the guard and said, "I have an urgent matter for the king, and you must let me in immediately."
The guard repeated what Gandhini had said and then let him pass. Gandhini went by without lowering the candle.
"Then you must gather all the commanders at the city square."

The guard immediately ran off, and Gandhini rushed towards the palace. He had heard of wight candles before, that those who looked into the light were susceptible to commands, but he had never seen it in action and was relieved that it worked.

Gandhini swung open the large wooden doors to King Alberath's grand hall. He stepped onto the stone floor and looked across the room. There sat the king on his throne. On the steps below were some people in lavish clothing. The hall was dark except for a few torches placed on the floor. Long blue draperies with gold tassels hung along the sides.

Gandhini scrutinised the people sitting in front of the king. At first, he thought the king's jesters were sitting in a circle around the throne, but he was mistaken. These were the city's leading politicians having a meeting with the ruler. Two guards on either side of Gandhini lowered their halberds and pointed at him. Gandhini thought he had only one chance and spoke up, loud and clear.

"Outside the city walls are creatures from the underworld, they are heading east in pursuit of a dragon."

"A dragon?" laughed one of the jesters on the lowest step. "What kind of tales are you bringing us, old merchant?"

"We are not at liberty to listen at this moment; you must wait for a suitable opportunity." It was a woman who spoke, her voice revealing her gender. She was a figure of authority and was dressed like the other men. In essence, she was just like the other men, except that for genetic reasons, she could be called a woman.

Gandhini was about to raise his voice again, but the two guards ushered him out into the corridor. The doors closed, and he sat down to wait.

Late in the afternoon, the doors finally opened. Gandhini was irritated because the enemy army had gained a significant head start, but he didn't want to dwell on that now. He needed to convince the king and his politicians of the danger. Gandhini approached the authorities, who were indulging in the fruit platters arranged around the throne.
"There are goblins, trolls, and cabras, look, I have proof," said Gandhini, carefully taking out the knife and the wight candles. The king perked up his ears when he heard the candles mentioned and looked into Gandhini's eyes. He was a wise king with extensive experience, a good listener, which was something different from the politicians at his feet. Everyone in the room except the king stared at the wight candles.
"You must help me convince the king that the enemy is in the country," shouted Gandhini, and immediately everyone began to turn towards the king, eager to persuade him that the land was occupied.
"Silence," roared the king. "East, you say?" said the king thoughtfully. "In the castle Dawnfall by the sea lives my son, Prince Robert. Let the man speak."

Gandhini now detailed his entire story about his friends traveling east. He deliberately omitted any mention of Heart the mountain, thinking it might be too much to

believe, even though he knew the tale of the mountain would be significant. He spoke about the goblins and how he had seen the large army outside the city. He was a skilled storyteller, and now everyone believed him. He had long since put away the wight candles.
There was a knock on the door, and a soldier entered the hall.
"You must come outside. A vast army stands outside the city walls," he said convincingly.

At the city square, all the military commanders had gathered in the morning. They didn't know why and discussed for a long time the reason for their assembly. Later in the day, they learned of the approaching army and began to prepare the city's defence.

The king now stepped out onto the wall, accompanied by his officials. They looked out over the immense army that had gathered around the city. Gandhini was also present and quickly noticed that this was a different force than the one the dragon had spoken of. This was not trolls and cabras, these were ordinary soldiers, human soldiers.
A golden dragon came flying towards the city, and everyone immediately raised their weapons.
"Stop," shouted Gandhini,

Chapter 18:
The Great Battle

Mephistor reveled in every second, at last, he would kill the despised dragon. He couldn't decide what was best: the feeling that he was about to slay the dragon, the actual moment of killing it, or knowing that the last dragon was slain and annihilated. All three were equally vile, but he enjoyed the first the most; it was a wonderful thought to know that the dragon would soon die. Mephistor was now approaching the wind bridge and could see the dragon atop the wall.
"Your end is near!" he said, laughing loudly.

The trumpet blasts from the crest came unexpectedly. On both sides of Heart, there were soldiers as far as the eye could see. There were also knights in shining armour. Prince Robert knew they hadn't called for reinforcements; they hadn't had the opportunity. Even if they had managed to send a message, it would have taken days for anyone to mobilise and come to their aid. Moreover, he didn't recognise any military force that could stand against this army of monsters; the enemy was too powerful.
No one knew which army stood on the crest, but everyone hoped they were not the enemy's. The mountain had now

moved aside, and soldiers ran along the road, striking at the beasts as they descended.

The breach created by Heart allowed mounted soldiers to quickly descend onto the battlefield, creating chaos among the goblins and cabras. The horses came like a second landslide, pouring over Mephistor's army, which was scattered.

The soldiers in the castle gained extra courage when they realised it was their allies who had arrived, and they began to beat back the cabras that had tried to open the gate. The trolls in the moat roared, trying to get the monsters to turn back. They were now under attack instead of being the attackers.

Prince Robert Wenchester stood atop the wall, unable to comprehend the nature of this army. Not even his father, King Alberath, had so many soldiers. Where had they all come from?

There was no time to ponder this now. The prince struck at the remaining cabras inside the courtyard. They were confused by the trolls' orders to turn back and didn't know where to go. After a while, the courtyard was cleared, and those remaining on the wall were cut down as they tried to flee.

"Open the gate," commanded the prince, gathering a troop to follow him out. Gecko wanted to join, under the protection of Tom, of course. Art also joined, along with a score of mounted riders.

The prince mounted his steed and rode out. Out on the wind bridge, the prince and his knights encountered lost cabras. They slew many and then continued onto the battlefield. Some trolls, realising they could not fight on two fronts, gathered the nearest beasts and counterattacked. When they saw the dragon, they went berserk, screaming, "Kill the dragon."

Art breathed fire like never before. He had always believed that his riches were what made him a fire-breathing dragon. Now, he had no treasure, but he had great friends, and he had found the love of his life. His flame was now more intense than ever.
The dragon's fire confused the enemy, giving the soldiers the chance to deliver lethal blows. This technique proved highly effective; the dragon, along with the prince and five soldiers, killed hundreds of cabras in this way.

The prince looked out over the battlefield again. The army that had come to their aid was still cut off, with the majority of the field swarming with enemies. He could see the king's standard, the white with the blue elephant, but there were also other flags, one red with a golden dragon.

Sir Notalot charged directly into the enemy ranks, creating chaos. He was like an island in a sea of foes. Moving along the rear of the frontline, he disrupted the cabras, easing the battle for the fighting soldiers. When the armoured figure burst into a group of enemies, the cabras and goblins jumped aside in terror at his approach. Sometimes they landed on each other, and sometimes they inadvertently leaped among soldiers who, with swords drawn, struck at them. After Tom passed, it was as if an invisible force reshaped the enemy lines, quickly reforming them into a strong front.

Mephistor, a formidable warlord, used flames and lightning to annihilate everything in his path; nothing could hold him back. Art attacked and momentarily weakened him, just as he had done with the cabras. Spears were thrown and arrows shot, but they all merely bounced off him.
"No one can kill me!" he bellowed, lunging towards the dragon. Art responded with immense flames, stalling the assault for a brief moment. The black general fell to his knees. His fur was burned away, and his skin was red and black, but it seemed to hardly affect him. Quickly, Mephistor was back on his feet, lunging once more at the dragon.

Sir Notalot, accustomed to his enemies fleeing from him, charged forward, believing that the Dread Emperor would also halt. He rushed forward and performed his renowned gesture, but the warlord did not care; he didn't even notice him. Tom witnessed up close how Mephistor overwhelmed Art with his full arsenal. This was the last real adversary for Mephistor, the only one who could harm him now and in the future. The dragon was now completely paralysed, and Mephistor sensed victory; the dragon would finally die.

The sword pierced Mephistor's back and thrust through his evil heart, continuing out through his chest. Mephistor looked down in surprise at the bloody sword tip, feeling immense pain. Slowly, he turned around. He saw a man in armour and could not comprehend how this was possible; he was supposed to be immortal.
"No human can kill me!" he said as if it would help him, as if it would reverse what had happened and some higher power would rewind his life for a moment. But that was all he managed to say before he fell dead. Tom had physically picked up a sword from the ground and thrust it through Mephistor in a last attempt to save his friend. He had to do something; he couldn't just watch his best friend be killed. He succeeded, and he was the only one who could do it. Sir Notalot was something else, neither human nor animal, something Mephistor didn't know existed.

With Mephistor's fall, a shockwave seemed to pass through the battlefield. The enemy forces, now leaderless, began to falter. The defenders, buoyed by this unexpected turn of events, redoubled their efforts. The tide of battle had shifted dramatically. Sir Notalot, standing over Mephistor's lifeless body, had not only saved his friend but also changed the course of the battle. As the enemy's ranks broke and retreated, the defenders rallied, pushing back the dark forces that had threatened their city and the entire realm. The great battle was nearing its conclusion, a conclusion that now promised hope and victory.

Art quickly recovered and looked approvingly at Tom. They could hear a cheer as if all the soldiers had followed the event, but the applause came from another direction. Art and Tom looked around and managed to locate the source of the joyous shouts at the crest. Over the ridge, a golden dragon was flying in. The armoured dragon swooped down over the enemy and followed the front line. From its mouth spewed powerful flames that washed over the enemy's front line. After the dragon passed, soldiers rushed forward and killed all the weakened cabras. The dragon swung out over the sea, turned, and dived again towards the enemy.
Art sighed, "She is indeed beautiful."

The enemy forces quickly collapsed, surrounded and forming a semicircle with the sea at their back. Many cabras and other beasts were thrown over the edge. These creatures had never seen the sea before; they couldn't swim, and if they didn't smash against the rocks, they quickly drowned. The trolls surrendered and lay down on the ground. The beasts didn't know whom to fight when the trolls ceased commanding. Some cabras began attacking each other. The war finally seemed to be drawing to an end.

The few surviving trolls were forced to keep the herd calm and still until the war tribunal decided what to do with the prisoners of war. Art was overjoyed to see Philomenia again; he had thought he would never see her again.

Philomenia and Art, in the final phase of the battle, fought side by side, and never before had anyone seen such flames. Their combined strength and the unity they displayed were a sight to behold, a testament to the power of camaraderie and love in the face of adversity. The great battle was over, and though the cost was high, the victory was a significant one, marking the beginning of a new era of peace and hope for the realm.

Philomenia's castle in the west began to experience visits from ominous creatures not long after Art, Tom, Gecko, and the mountain had departed. Initially, her soldiers, who were well-trained, encountered these attacks in the fields. They had no significant trouble repelling these initial skirmishes, but the frequency and intensity of the attacks grew. Soon, cabras and goblins began appearing at the gates, provoking and threatening that entire armies would come and slaughter everyone.

The soldiers successfully captured some goblins and coerced them into revealing stories about the apocalypse, the cruel ruler Mephistor, and other horrors. They also learned that all the monstrous creatures were emerging from a single location, a passage to the underworld. This passage had been opened when a colossal rock had dislodged and rolled away. Philomenia realised the significance of the mountain and the importance of getting her back in place.

Resolved to take action, Philomenia decided to gather her army and come to the aid of her friends. Art had become everything to her, and she could not bear the thought of losing him. With this determination, she began to mobilise her forces, preparing them for the journey and the battles that might lie ahead.

Philomenia's decision was not just a personal one; it was also strategic. Closing the passage to the underworld was crucial to preventing further invasions and ensuring the safety of her realm and the neighbouring lands. Her army, skilled and loyal, rallied to her call, ready to embark on this vital mission.

Marching in a wide formation, they neutralised every enemy they encountered. All the goblins and cabras seemed to be heading east, as if some invisible force was directing them. This was troubling, yet it also justified her decision to leave the castle with minimal guard. It seemed unlikely that any harm would come to it while they were away.
Following the path carved by Heart, Philomenia and her soldiers approached another of its creations by the afternoon: the new bridge over the Trip River. They were amazed by the bridge, recognising its potential to revolutionise trade and future cooperation between lands. "If there are any lands left to trade with," Philomenia thought sombrely, considering the widespread chaos.

They swiftly crossed the Perghoola Plain, heading towards Mount Dragon, moving along the path now dubbed by the soldiers as the "Heart's Way." The name was a fitting tribute to the massive changes the mountain had brought to the landscape.

Even on the other side of the bridge, they encountered goblins and cabras, now in larger groups often led by a troll. These battles were more challenging; not just due to the trolls' leadership, but there was something else. The goblins that had harassed the castle seemed like mere bandits compared to these formidable warriors. Their increased coordination and aggression suggested a heightened level of organisation and possibly a direct influence from a higher command.

They followed the Path of the Heart when it turned north and after many days of walking, they arrived one afternoon at Wyrmville. The village appeared deserted at first glance. Windows were boarded up, some houses were burned down to mere heaps of ash, fences were broken, and chicken coops stood empty. The fields, once cultivated, were now overrun with weeds, a clear sign that no one tended to the land anymore.

As they passed through the main street, all the soldiers looked around in wonder at the tragic state of the buildings. Movement caught their eye from behind the planks of a window. Doors began to open slowly behind them, and a window on the other side of the street cracked

open. A woman stepped out onto the street. Her clothes were tattered, and she seemed extremely distraught. She struggled to remain standing, her legs looked ready to bolt at any moment.
"What are you doing here? There's nothing left to take," she said, trying to sound assertive.
The poorly-dressed woman, the town's mayor, had indeed faced harrowing times. Her village, once thriving on the fringes of the dragon's treasure, was now almost completely desolate. The village had been self-sufficient with its farming, and the dragon's payments for various services had been a significant secondary income for the villagers. But now, nearly everything was ruined by cabras, goblins, and trolls. The dragon was gone, and even the mountain had mysteriously vanished, leaving the villagers without their main source of prosperity and protection.
The mayor's eyes widened in surprise as she caught sight of the dragon queen. The presence of another dragon, especially one of such stature, was completely unexpected for her. She had met the dragon in the cave a few times before, but the idea of encountering another dragon had never crossed her mind. She greeted her respectfully, upon which the dragon introduced itself.
"I am queen Philomenia, ruler of the land of Faroon. This is my army. We are looking for the dragon that used to live here in the mountain." Philomenia spoke about what had happened and her desire to see the entrance to the underworld.

"Of course, follow me," said the woman, leading the way to where Mount Dragon once stood. The rest of the villagers, now feeling braver, emerged onto the street and most followed cautiously behind.
As the sun began to set, they arrived at the hole. The villagers crept carefully to the edge and looked down. The ground sloped steeply downward, ending in a black abyss. When the soldiers arrived, they lined the rim of the ravine, and soon the entire chasm was surrounded by multiple layers of soldiers. The dragon queen stood inside the ring of soldiers, looking down at the hole with disdain.

Suddenly, a troll emerged from the hole, causing the villagers to recoil in fright. The soldiers swiftly drew their swords as the troll launched an attack, clumsily running up the slope towards the queen. It leapt forward in an attempt to strike, but before it could reach her, it fell dead. Arrows had flown in from all directions, striking the troll with deadly accuracy.
"The dragon queen realised that there was little more they could do here than to prevent more monsters from coming up through the hole. She left a troop of skilled archers to guard it so that no more creatures would enter this part of the world. Philomenia looked respectfully at the villagers and then turned to the mayor.
'We will put the mountain back in its place here,' she said very firmly, and both the archers and the villagers felt reassured upon hearing her decision."

The villagers informed them that the monsters had begun to move south towards the capital, Hagriven, apparently preparing for a major assault. There were also rumours among the villagers that Mephistor, the ruler of the underworld, had arrived and was gathering an army of all the monsters to destroy everything and everyone. This news was alarming, and Philomenia decided to set off for the south immediately. The most capable men and women of Wyrmville formed a small troop that also joined them. This was a matter of great importance to them, and even though they were not soldiers, they hoped to contribute in some way to the fight against the underworld.

Philomenia hastened her troops, and only two days after leaving Wyrmville, they could see Hagriven on the horizon. They moved slowly, constantly vigilant, aware that enemies could be anywhere around them.
As they drew closer to the city, no monsters or enemies were in sight. Stealthily, they spread out, forming an invisible ring around the city. They slowly closed the circle, combing through the forests until only the city walls remained. They could now see soldiers on the wall staring at them in terror. Philomenia decided to fly into the city to find out what had happened to Mephistor and his monster army. Where had the dreadful force gone?

Philomenia was alarmed to discover that the entire city was prepared for an attack and was ready to defend itself. She had thousands of archers below her, all with arrows on their drawn bows, all pointed at her. She closed her eyes first, a foolish reflex to erase the sight before her. Realising she had to turn back, suddenly all the archers lowered their bows. She saw a man waving from the wall and swooped down to greet him.

Gandhini was the one who had waved, and he was also the one who recognised the army that had surrounded the city. He knew the dragon queen and was able to clear up any misunderstandings. The king gathered everyone in his hall, where all the officials had differing opinions about the situation. They had various viewpoints and primarily wanted to highlight their own importance, rather than what was best for the country. The king knew this and relied more on Gandhini. The dragon queen also got along very well with the king, and they decided to head to Dawnfall together with both armies.

They both had someone there whom they loved and valued highly.

Chapter 19:

Heart's Final Rest

Once again, the Dragon Queen wandered up the slope to the place where the mountain had once stood. This time, she was accompanied by King Alberath, Art, Tom, Gecko, and of course, Heart, the mountain herself. Earlier in the day, the rest of the enemy army had been driven back into the hole, and now the queen's archers stood very proud in a circle around the large crater.

The soldiers cheered and raised their weapons as Heart slowly glided up the hill to settle in the vast hollow. Gone was the angry mountain they had come to know. Heart was calm and enjoyed a bit of the attention it received. It had discovered friends and was beginning to almost regret its decision to forever settle in the pit. When it reached the edge and saw the hole to the underworld, the hole from which all the monsters had come, it realised that it had to take its place.

This was what it had wished for when it had set out on its journey several weeks ago. "I am ready," it said and continued the last bit over the pit. To everyone's surprise, it fit perfectly into the indentation. There was no seam or edge. It was hard to imagine that there had been a large hole here just a moment ago.

Heart relaxed and looked at Art, Tom, and Gecko. "Thank you for everything. You can disconnect me now," she said and closed her eyes. Art ran up the mountain. He had been to the summit once before, when they rode together towards Dawnfall Castle. He had also lived in the mountain for hundred years, so he was very familiar with it, and it felt like saying goodbye to a very dear old friend. Art opened the bottle and began to sprinkle around when Tom started waving his arms and Gecko shouted from the foot of the mountain, "Save some of the content for Sir Notalot." Art didn't understand what Gecko meant at first, but then he realised that Tom is alive in the same way as the mountain. Perhaps Tom also wanted to end his life by pouring the magical liquid over himself. He stopped and looked at the contents; there was still a little left at the bottom. He began to walk back down the mountain and felt life disappearing from the ground, how the mountain beneath him stopped vibrating. It was like the warmth was disappearing. Then everything became still and quiet. Art thought of Heart's dull voice and her curses, overturned cobblestones, and moraine rot.

Heart was now gone, she had petrified, her eyes were no longer visible, her rumbling had quieted. They could all see the mountain in front of them, but they felt that she was no longer there. Silently, they left the place. Gecko looked for a crevice or something similar where the mouth had been. He had planned to crawl in and look for gold, but it felt so wrong now that Heart was no more.

He found no opening, but he saw something else strange. It was as if the mountain had formed a vessel where the mouth had previously been. At first, Gecko thought it looked like she was sticking out her tongue, but it was a sort of indentation. "Wait," said Gecko and ran over to the protruding formation. He quickly climbed along the side of the mountain and looked down into the bowl. There lay a few gold coins. Gecko picked them up, guessing that Heart had left them for him.

Henceforth, visitors could sometimes find coins in Heart's bowl. It was as if the bowl knew who was looking into it, and for those who already had enough, it was always empty. Many were the disappointed fortune-seekers who traveled to the mountain in vain, but some found a coin, just as much as they needed.

When the entire company passed through Wyrmville, Tom couldn't help but feel sorry for these people. They had suffered the most, and Tom decided that his little treasure would go towards rebuilding the small village. Gecko also wanted to contribute, and they gathered the village and announced the new construction fund. The mayor received the gift, which would be used to build houses and barns. The inhabitants of Wyrmville cheered and gained new hope for the future. Gecko suggested that they would also need an inn, as there will be many traveller wanting to visit Mount Dragon, or rather, The Heart's Summit, which had become its new name.

It had been a long hike but when they finally approached Philomenia's castle, Art wanted to take a look from the cliff. He vividly remembered how fascinated he had been the first time he saw the castle. He hadn't been at that height since then and wanted to reawaken that old memory. Philomenia and the soldiers followed the path while Art, Tom, and Gecko went to view the panorama.

They reached the cliff, and Art was stunned again, but this time it wasn't the castle that amazed him, but what he saw at the gates. The place was swarming with trolls, goblins, and other monsters. The castle was under siege. He couldn't see any of the defenders on the wall and wondered what was happening.

He slung Sir Notalot and Gecko onto his back and started running towards the castle. He roared through the forest to Philomenia and her soldiers. "They're attacking the castle!" he bellowed. They all arrived simultaneously at the winding road down to the castle. They could see loads of slain cabras lying at the bridgehead and on the bridge. Dead and injured goblins and trolls were strewn all the way down. In the river below, Art saw crocodiles fighting over prey that had fallen down recently. Philomenia was worried that her defenders had come to harm. "I should have left more soldiers behind to guard the castle."

They could see the trolls attacking the gate, only to fall dead, often tumbling over the edge into the river, as if there was some invisible defence of the castle.

Two large trolls blocked the path as Art and some soldiers came running. Art flared up, forcing the trolls to shield their faces. In that moment, the soldiers rushed forward and attacked with their spears. Soon, the trolls lay dead before them. They stepped over the bodies and chased after some goblins fleeing down the road. The goblins quickly realised there was no escape route and leaped over the edge, hoping for better luck with the crocodiles.

Gecko looked towards the castle and shouted, "There are Limberiks on the wall!" He had spotted Jamarar and his friends up there.
Many arm-length folk were stationed on the wall, expertly hurling stones with remarkable precision. They aimed with deadly accuracy, striking the eyes of the trolls or the heads of the goblins. One cabras was hit squarely in the eye, becoming so disoriented that it stumbled over the edge, plummeting down to be swiftly claimed by a waiting crocodile in the river below.

As Art, Tom, and all of Philomenia's soldiers launched their surprise attack from the rear, it did not take long for the tide of battle to turn decisively. One by one, the invaders were either slain or forced to leap into the river in a desperate attempt to escape. The battlefield quickly cleared, leaving a grim scene of victory.

Meanwhile, Philomenia was fraught with worry for the soldiers she had left behind to guard the castle. Having not seen any sign of them, she feared the worst, believing they might have all perished valiantly defending the fortress. However, as she entered the castle's courtyard, her anxiety gave way to immense relief and joy. To her astonishment and gratitude, she was warmly greeted by all of the soldiers she had feared lost. Their survival and the defence they had mounted against overwhelming odds filled Philomenia with immense pride and relief. Seeing them safe and sound was a heartening moment, bringing a rare smile to her face amid the aftermath of the fierce battle.

The soldiers recounted that when all their arrows and spears had been exhausted, the arm-length folk had appeared as if out of nowhere. At first, they mistook them for small goblins that had found a back way into the castle, but they soon realised these were skilled Limberiks, capable of hurling stones with remarkable precision. The soldiers had then adapted their strategy, and over the past few days, they had been supplying the Limberiks with stones. This was why they hadn't been visible from the outside, and the soldiers themselves hadn't realised that help was so close at hand.

Philomenia was quick to express her gratitude to the Limberiks for their critical intervention. She declared that from that day forward, they would be an integral part of

the castle's defence. She generously offered them the freedom to move about the castle as they pleased, recognising their valiant contribution and the role they had played in saving the fortress from what could have been a catastrophic defeat. This decision not only reinforced the castle's defences but also fostered a sense of unity and camaraderie among all those who called the castle home. Philomenia's swift and inclusive response highlighted her wisdom and leadership, qualities that endeared her to her people and her allies alike.
"You can live in the castle," she said, but Jamarar firmly replied that Limberiks prefer to live in caves. It ended with them being offered help if they wanted to remodel.
"Thank you, that would be great. The crocodiles can sometimes be a bit too bold," Jamarar replied cheerfully.

In the weeks following their return home, things began to settle down. Art found himself becoming more familiar with the castle's layout and started to get to know the soldiers. It turned out they held great respect for him. They had fought side by side, and everyone was impressed by the courage Art had displayed on the battlefield.

New passageways and entrances were constructed to facilitate easier access for the Limberiks. Jamarar and his friends were now able to move freely within the castle, but they often chose to stay in their caves near the water. These new pathways not only symbolised the integration of the Limberiks into the castle community but also

reflected the evolving dynamics of the castle's defences. The soldiers and arm-length folk, having forged bonds through shared experiences in battle, now worked together to strengthen the fortifications and prepare for any future threats, all while maintaining the unique character and traditions of their respective groups.
One evening, Art found himself wondering about Tom's whereabouts. He realised he hadn't seen his friend for several days. Starting to feel concerned, Art began to inquire amongst those around the castle, but to his growing unease, nobody knew where Tom was; no one had seen him.

Art's worry deepened, fearing that Tom might have done something reckless. He remembered leaving the half-empty bottle with Tom after using most of its contents on Heart. Art knew that the bottle belonged to Tom and that he had the right to decide its use, but there was a lingering concern that Tom might wish to end his life, just as the mountain had.

As Art's thoughts spiralled, his concern intensified. "Tom can't just vanish; he's my best friend," he thought anxiously. He embarked on a thorough search, exploring every conceivable and inconceivable space within the castle. He delved into the areas occupied by the Limberiks and even ventured up to the cliff that overlooked the castle, a place known for its sweeping views. Gecko joined in the search, equally clueless about Tom's whereabouts over the past few days. Their shared concern brought them together in this urgent quest. Tom seemed to have disappeared without a trace, leaving Art and Gecko to search tirelessly, fuelled by their deep bond of friendship and the hope that Tom was still somewhere to be found, safe and sound.

Late in the evening, Art and Gecko were completely exhausted after their extensive search. Searching is tiring enough, but the added strain of worrying about one's best friend makes it even more gruelling. Art and Gecko were thoroughly drained when they entered Art's bedroom that night.

It was then they discovered Sir Notalot, standing motionless against the wall, just inside the door. On the floor in front of him lay the bottle, now empty. Art was struck with horror and began to cry. "You could have at least said goodbye," he sobbed. "Not just sneak away like this and disappear." In a burst of emotion, Art grabbed the empty bottle and hurled it against the wall, where it shattered with a loud crash. "You old faithful tin can, why would you do this?" Art sighed deeply, enveloping the armour in a heartfelt embrace.

Suddenly, Tom stirred, waking up and turning his head. Gecko immediately hopped in through the visor. "He's just been resting," Gecko explained. "But why here, in my room?" Art wondered, still confused and overwhelmed.

Gecko then revealed that Tom had spent the last few days with an old suit of armour that had helped him the last time they were being pursued in the castle. This armour, like Tom, was also sentient. It had stood in that corridor for over a hundred years. To Tom, it had recounted its experiences, the wars it had been compelled to participate in, and the subsequent peace, a time when it no longer served any purpose. This interaction had provided Tom with a sense of kinship and understanding, a connection to another being who had shared a similarly unique and often challenging existence.

After sharing the story of its life with Sir Notalot, the sentient armour requested the remaining contents of the bottle. This request aligned with what Tom had been considering when he asked Art to save some of the liquid. Moved by the incredible tale it had shared, Tom went to Art's bedroom, knowing it was a place where he could rest undisturbed.

"We thought you had poured the bottle over yourself," Art sighed, embracing Tom so tightly it almost left dents. "Easy there!" Gecko called out from inside the armour. "Tom plans that when the time comes to end his existence, he'll choose a much more celebratory spot than your bedroom.".

THE END

Thank you for taking the time to read my book.
You can contact me at http://www.gadnell.com/en

Stefan Gadnell

www.ingramcontent.com/pod-product-compliance
Lightning Source LLC
LaVergne TN
LVHW041207150826
845673LV00001B/314

9789198940220